THE INNER CITY

KAREN HEULER

ChiZine Publications

FIRST EDITION

The Inner City © 2012 by Karen Heuler
Cover artwork © 2012 by Erik Mohr
Interior design © 2012 by Samantha Beiko
Author photo © Tracey Sides Photography
All Rights Reserved.

978-1-927469-33-0

Distributed in Canada by
HarperCollins Canada Ltd.
1995 Markham Road
Scarborough, ON M1B 5M8
Toll Free: 1-800-387-0117
e-mail: hcorder@harpercollins.com

Distributed in the U.S. by
Diamond Book Distributors
1966 Greenspring Drive
Timonium, MD 21093
Phone: 1-410-560-7100 x826
e-mail: books@diamondbookdistributors.com

Library and Archives Canada Cataloguing in Publication

Available upon request

CHIZINE PUBLICATIONS
Toronto, Canada
www.chizinepub.com
info@chizinepub.com

Edited and copyedited by Stephen Michell
Proofread by Samantha Beiko

Canada Council   Conseil des Arts
for the Arts   du Canada

We acknowledge the support of the Canada Council for the Arts which last year
invested $20.1 million in writing and publishing throughout Canada.

ONTARIO ARTS COUNCIL
CONSEIL DES ARTS DE L'ONTARIO
50 YEARS OF ONTARIO GOVERNMENT SUPPORT OF THE ARTS
50 ANS DE SOUTIEN DU GOUVERNEMENT DE L'ONTARIO AUX ARTS

Published with the generous assistance of the Ontario Arts Council.

Printed in Canada

THE
INNER
CITY

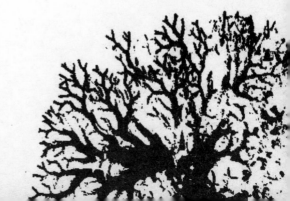

Contents

FishWish

Celia picked up a whole fish at the market, and she laid it out on the cutting board when she got home and looked at it closely. It had golden gills and silver fins, and copper scales and garnet eyes. "You're quite beautiful," she said. "I never noticed how beautiful a fish was before."

"Don't eat me," the fish cried. "Throw me back in the sea and I will give you what you want."

"I'll do it," she said, "because you're beautiful and I don't wish to see you die."

She wrapped the fish up and took the subway to Coney Island, which was dark with rain and empty because of the chill. She walked along the boardwalk until she saw a pier and then walked out to the end, where the wind whipped the sea up into whitecaps and greencaps. She knelt down and unwrapped her fish, whose scales were brighter because it was near the sea. The garnet eyes turned ruby and hypnotic, the scales shone and the fins flashed and she felt as if she were riding the waves, rushing up and rushing down.

She had felt this way once before. "I can't let you go," she said. "I'm in love with you."

"I will give you three wishes if you let me go," the fish said. "It's the lure of wishing that you mistake for love. Beware of lures; I myself keep mistaking hooks for love."

"Three wishes?" she said, drawing back on her knees. Her eyes looked out at the water, which rose and swelled towards her; everything was coming towards her.

"I don't know what to wish for," she said.

"It's easy as can be. Wish for wealth, wish for purpose, wish for love," the fish cajoled her.

"But which is better?" she wondered. "Wealth or purpose or love? Or I could wish for immortality. Or something else I can't quite think of now, that will seem to me so obvious later on. I'm always thinking of things later on."

"You don't have forever," the fish said, and it flashed its scales and thrilled its fins. "There's a time limit, as there is in everything. You have only two more hours, and then I'll die and the wishes will die too. Do you want me to die?"

She lowered her head and closed her eyes. "Oh no, dear fish, I won't let you die. I'll wish for something by then; I'll think of something, I swear. But for now, for now, I want to look at you and hold you and think of everything you can promise me." And she picked the fish up and held it to her chest and began to walk back down the pier and onto the sand and along the shore, where the water rushed around her ankles and threatened to knock her down.

"Be careful," cried the fish. "Drop me in the water, not the sand. I can't live in the sand."

She let the water wash around her ankles. She loved the feel of it, the way it lunged at her and wanted her.

"This is the happiest I've been, with the waves at my legs and the roar of the water and the sound of your voice. This is what I crave, I think; I'm happy now."

"You don't have much time left," the fish said. "If you don't release me I shall die and all your wishes will too. Think of what you want. Ask for what your heart craves. What do you want most of all?"

Celia looked at the waves and looked at the fish in her arms. "I want to be you," she said. "Why not be what I love the most? I wish to be you!"

At that her body stumbled back against the sand and the fish leaped from her arms and dove into the ocean. At once Celia felt the waves against her like a beautiful wall parting. I am a fish! she cried to herself and opened her mouth and wiggled her tail and plunged forward, her heart pumping wildly. Around her everything moved slipping around and up and down, silvering, pointing, scuttling. How extraordinary the sea is, she thought, because it was crowded with life, schools of fish, gnarled heads behind shells and rocks, long snouts and broad snouts. I must be careful, she thought; what kind of fish am I after all—am I good to eat? I should have asked.

She swam low where the water was coolest, but steered away from shadows where eyes and teeth might hide. Farther out, she slipped in among the schools of fish that rippled around her like skirts of fish, clouds of fish, shelves of fish, filling up the water. She picked up speed, just enjoying the momentum of being one in the pattern of fish, following the fish movements around her, quick drops, quick turns, the irresistible dash after a dash beside her. There was such a deep pleasure in it, in the riding of impulse, in the deciphering of sensation, although she was beginning to feel something else, a deep-rooted wish for, desire for . . . and then a small fish raced past her and she opened her mouth and gulped.

It glanced against her throat! She could feel a last wriggle in her gut! Even now she felt it swill around with the burst of water she'd taken, and there was no remorse! This was right, and this was so. She looked around at the school of fish moving away from her, darting industriously, and she caught the nervous stare of their fish eyes on her, round and focused, and it was an immense feeling, a new feeling, righteous and benign even as the little gasp within her died.

Fortified, she swam forward, moving to left and right, sighting future meals and watching for what might be dangerous. She knew there must be danger because new motions caused her to jump away from them, shadows from above caused an instant panic; reefs disturbed her with their possibilities in nooks and caverns. She saw, far off, creatures heading for her.

She thought: I know my second wish. It is to be a bigger fish, and she was stunned by the rightness of it, and how silly she had been not to think of it. A large fish, she thought, I know its name, I know its speed and the sharpness of its teeth, now what is it called again? She chased a small fish and gulped it. What is it called? I will merely say, I wish to be a larger fish, with larger teeth, and that will be it, she thought. Now I must go back and ask for the wish.

She flicked her tail easily, leaning into her fin and slicing through the water as if it were air—easier than air, much easier. She twitched to the left and then to the right, keeping her body in a curve, and she felt a great sense of power until she saw a bigger fish scattering other fish before him, and she remembered she must get back to the shore and ask for her second wish before it was too late.

She raced, then, flicking her head left and right, scooting down and then up to keep in sight all the directions where bigger fish could come for her.

She loved the way her body bent and moved, quick and accurate, and delighted in the look of a smaller fish as it drove away or as she caught it automatically, soothed by the feel of its ultimate wriggle. She hastened now back to the beach, to the sands where she had parted from her old life and become the fish. She expected it to be waiting there, for her, waiting to hear her second wish, and as she surfaced once or twice, locating herself along the first pier, and then following the trail she had taken along the sand, she saw her old body propped up against a piling, staring blankly at the ocean, and she leaped as far as she could leap into the air in recognition.

"I wish to be bigger!" she cried. "I wish to be as big as the biggest, sharpest fish! This is my second wish!" and she dropped herself down again in the water and wriggled closer to the shore, but not too close because it was shallow and as a bigger fish she might get stranded, even a fish with sharper teeth.

Of course size was relative, and she might already be a bigger fish, so she surfaced again, her eye above the water peering at her old body; she seemed no closer or farther than when she had announced her wish; she seemed no bigger or smaller. "My second wish!" she cried again, but the body propped up along the piling had no answer for her and she crept a little closer, rocked by the narrowness of the waves.

Her old self leaned limply and had no sparkle, no lustre

at all. Her old body was drab and knobby and graceless; she didn't miss it; all she thought of was getting her second wish and being off again.

"My wish!" she insisted and spun around in the shallows, ploughing up a massive splash of water to wake the nasty thing against the piling. The waves she made rushed towards it and it spilled over, fell over, into the shallows and she thought with relief that *that* would wake it, the ugly thing, but instead it lay there, washing a little back and forth as the sea came in and took a long scrape of water back out with it.

"My wish!" she cried again even then realizing what it was, that thing upon the beach, a dead thing creeping towards her with the backwash of the waves. "My second wish!" she cried again, furious that she had been so baldly cheated of a chance to be bigger, and sharper, and faster, and grim.

She swam up to it and nipped its lips; she wove around it and bit its chin. She nudged the eyes and flipped her tail between its hands, but all to no avail.

And while she swam back and forth, a bird swooped down at her and cried, "Another wish! I want another wish!" and she swam furiously away from it and away from its vile beak, nearing a yacht with a young man at the helm who called: "I know my third wish now, I want a seaplane, not a yacht, with golden wings and pearly seats, I want it now," and he turned the boat and headed for Celia, who wriggled back ahead of him, getting close again to the shore, where another woman called out, "Fish, fish! You promised me a life of wealth and beauty but I am not happy, fish. That's the last wish I have, I wish for happiness for I cannot go on like this, in misery!"

THE INNER CITY

And Celia darted back and forth, trying to escape the cries of wishes all around her. Was it too much to ask, to have her wishes first and foremost? Was it too much to ask, to be relieved of all this urgent chatter? She raised her own cries to the wind: "My second wish! My second wish!" she cried, and all around her other wishes raised their voices too and came at her with hooks and nets and the willful madness of desire.

THE INNER CITY

Lena Shayton is reading the newspaper, looking for a job, when she hears a knock on her door. It's the guy who lives below her, on the first floor. He wants to know if her apartment is shrinking. He has a notebook with measurements in it, and he says his apartment on the first floor is getting smaller each month. Is hers?

She considers the possibilities. If it's a come-on line, it's interesting. If he's serious, he's either artistic or crazy. This might be the way to make a new friend, which is what she needs right now. The love of her life, Bill, left her for Denise; she just lost her programming job; and there's a bad smell in the kitchen that she hasn't been able to track down.

Maybe it's the sewage treatment plant; the paper says there's a problem there that no one seems able to fix. Maybe it's Bill; maybe there's some weird thing happening where Bill tried to crawl back to her, got stuck under the sink, and died. But it's not likely; what would he be doing under the sink?

She lives over on Weehawken Street, which is a block from the river, at the westernmost part of the

West Village. She read in a book that in the old days of New York, Weehawken Street was almost on the river, before the landfill added another street. There used to be tunnels from Weehawken to the docks, for smuggling. She doesn't remember what they smuggled, but it adds to the possibility that Bill might have taken some sneaky secret way into her apartment and gotten stuck and died. She used to be the kind of person who wouldn't have thoughts like that, but now they give her pleasure.

She doesn't want to deal with this guy's mania. She tells him she measured yesterday, and it's definitely the same.

Lena goes through all the newspapers, looking for a job or for the inspiration for a job. There's a lot of news. Stuyvesant Town is complaining that their water pressure has practically disappeared; they coordinate shower schedules by floor.

The mayor warns the city of possible brownouts in the coming hot weather. Electrical usage is up 20% and has reached capacity. The mayor blames computers. "Turn off your printers," he demands. "Don't leave your computers on all the time. Conserve or we'll have an electric shortage like we once had a gas shortage. I'm not saying we're going to *ration* electricity out to people on alternating days like we did then." (And here, the reporter notes, his jaw got very firm.) "But we don't have infinite resources. If you blow the grid, it'll take a while to fix it."

Blow the grid! Lena thinks as she walks around the Village, and just because of all the fat and selfish people out there, the ones who take and give. Like the people who drop litter everywhere, which really annoys her. It doesn't take much to control litter—just put it in the trash cans on the corner. She sees a bunch of folders and papers beside an empty trash can, for instance. Some of it is even leaning against the empty can, that's how bad it is.

She picks up a handful of that paper. She tells herself that if she finds a name, she'll turn them in—however you do that, whoever you call. There's such a thing as accountability, after all. Though she's never "turned" anyone "in." Maybe it can't in fact be done. Nevertheless, she picks up a handful of papers.

It looks like someone's home office has been tidied up and dumped in the street. No, it must be a small business, because there's an inter-office memo from Harry Biskabit on garbage. "All paper must be shredded," it says. "We recently discovered some of our own letterhead fluttering down West Street. Needless to say, this could be disastrous. From now on, all paper of any kind must be brought to 151S3, where it will be listed, tallied, signed for and shredded before being put out. Foodstuffs and non-identifiable garbage can be handled as usual."

This is very funny, this guy Biskabit demanding that all the garbage be handled properly—and he can't handle his own!

A few memos look confidential. There's a job review and what looks like a warning about the poor work quality of someone named Philip Tarrey, who's always making mistakes and sending the wrong things to the wrong rooms. He's late with reports, he's poor at programming . . .

That's very interesting.

These papers could be a gold mine. They look a lot like a personnel file, and it looks like Philip Tarrey's been fired, and that means they need a programmer.

But who needs this programmer? She pages through the folder, finally finding some letterhead that reads "Assignment Specialties, 3 Charles Lane S3C, 77-33x14."

Charles Lane is only a few blocks away from where she stands. It's one block long, with a narrow cobblestone street running from Greenwich Avenue to West Street. There are blind storefronts along the southern side of the lane—concrete walls with steel doors. Trees with thin trunks press themselves against the walls. Everything on the north side is either a fenced-in garden or the back wall of row houses.

The only entrance doors are on the south side of the lane, but none of them have numbers. Where is 3 Charles Lane? Some kids come through on bicycles, followed by what she thinks might be NYU students doing something with cameras, posing each other and checking lighting. She can't find the address and there's no resident to ask.

Of course it's only three in the afternoon; maybe they're all at work with the doors closed. She decides to come back later, at five o'clock, and walks over to the park they're building by the river. They started about five years earlier, put in some trees, that kind of thing. It's nice for a block or two—there's even some grass and some bushes, but that seems to be all there is, despite all this talk about a pedestrian path going all the way uptown. Instead, there's mesh fencing blocking off the new paths, and lots of signs about construction. The signs are dirty; there's even a bush growing from construction debris.

At five, she wanders back, already half-convinced that the letterhead must be out of date. She turns the corner at West Street and stops—all along Charles Lane there are people in suits and dresses, with briefcases and shopping bags and coffee cups in their hands. They move rapidly up and down the lane, but they're eerily silent about it, not even their footsteps make a sound. But no doubt about it, they look like a commuter crowd, probably heading to the PATH train station just a few blocks away. It suddenly looks like Charles Lane is a thriving business artery. The buildings must be much deeper than they seem.

Everyone is coming out from one door, and when she gets there, she sees that it's actually a newsstand. She's so surprised that she walks in to get a better idea. At once, all the rush slows down. Lena stands still, looking around, and everyone inside seems to pause, picking up magazines or studying the sign above the counter for sodas and bottled waters. Lena sees a doorway marked "Employees Only," which has a dark curtain instead of a door. A man comes through, looks a little surprised, and then a small red light goes on over the doorway. She buys a soda and then leaves, joining the silent crowd outside as they walk to the end of the lane and disperse.

The only possibility she can think of is that this is a classified work place of some kind, maybe a secret government job, and the idea thrills her. She would like to do something dangerous or risky or at least more interesting than her usual. She pictures herself bluffing her way in, like a spy or counterspy. She's never done anything underhanded before; it's her turn. People are always taking advantage of her; let them watch out now.

Besides, it would be great to have a job that she could walk to. The subways are out of control right now with one accident after the other. The engineers say the signal lights are wrong; the maintenance people say the lights are fine. Trains crash into each other head to head or head to tail, it doesn't matter, she'd rather stay off them.

She wears an ironed blouse and a neat skirt the next morning and holds a briefcase with the papers she had picked up on the street, placed in a folder marked "Personal." On top of that she puts her resume, and on top of *that* she puts Harry Biskabit's memo. She gets to Charles Lane at 8:00 the next morning, and it's empty. There's one dog, one dog walker, and that's it. She's annoyed, because she's trying so hard to outsmart everyone and it doesn't seem to be working. The whole of Charles Lane has a blank, locked face. She touches the door where the newsstand was, and it's shut solid and looks suddenly like it never was open, never in its life. She goes over to the river again, looking out at the traffic jam. There are a few boats on the river. She's playing magic with herself. She's telling herself that when she turns around, she'll see Charles Lane bustling with life.

Then she turns around, and it is.

People are rushing around, back and forth. And there's a little café where the newsstand was. It even has an outside table and two chairs. Why would the stores be different at different times? Maybe it's some kind of new-wave timeshare scheme. Maybe on holidays it turns into a souvenir shop.

She merges with a wave of employees as they go through the café door. She steps behind two women, close behind, and to prove she's with them she starts matching their stride.

They go through the doorway marked Employees

Only. Lena keeps her head steady, trying not to look around too much. There's a short hallway and another curtain, with a guard on the other side. She bunches right up with the women ahead of her, almost stepping on their shoes, and she nods briskly. The guard grabs her.

"Your ID?" he asks.

"Job interview," she says. She opens her folder and flashes the letterhead. "See? Harry Biskabit. I have an appointment."

"You're supposed to have a temporary pass."

She rises to the occasion, scowling and huffing a little. "Now," she says, coldly, "how do I get a pass if I can't go in to get a pass?"

He blinks at her. "By mail?" he asks.

"You know they don't send them by mail. I was supposed to go in with those people you separated me from." She waves at the disappearing backs. "Hey, Juanita, you forgot me!" Then she pouts. "Now what?" She sighs in exasperation. "Can you call someone?"

He looks a little uncertain. "I just have instructions, you know. I don't need to justify everything I do, especially when it's regulation. But I do have discretion."

She smiles, suddenly friendly. "I've always admired discretion," she says. She's trying to mimic some sassy movie heroine from some gumshoe movie. She's getting a little jolt out of all the pretense.

He grins. "If you don't have an ID by tomorrow I'm gonna have to call in some backup."

"I understand," she says, giving him big eyes and then slipping by. "I'll make sure I get a good picture."

She takes a deep breath and keeps walking, fighting the impulse to slap someone on the back. She made it in!

Of course it's only a first step. She stops in the hallway to poke through her handbag, as if searching for a room number. When some more people come through, she falls in behind them.

They walk down a half-flight of steps, then through a short corridor to a bunch of elevators. Lena follows the others in and faces the buttons. S1, S2, S3. The others push S2. The memo from Biskabit says S3, so she pushes that. People come rushing in and by the time the doors close, the elevator's almost full. As soon as they shut, a murmur breaks out, as if they were suddenly allowed to speak.

"Did you see the new offices yet?" one man asks his neighbour.

"Katie's department moved in. They're still pushing for more storage, but it looks great. Not so crowded."

"We're next," the man says. "Can't wait." The doors open to S2 and they move out. That leaves just Lena and a slightly overweight man in a gray suit.

He smiles at her. "You new here?"

She's a little thrown by that. How can she sneak in if everyone can see she's new?

"I was behind you when the guard asked for your ID," he says. "Don't panic. I can't read minds."

"Phew," she says. "I thought maybe I had a sticker on me or something."

The elevator doors open and they both step out. Lena lets him lead the way.

"No, no, no, you look perfectly fine. Is this your first interview? Or is it a transfer?"

She's tempted to say transfer, it seems like the easy way out, but he would be sure to ask where she transferred from. "Interview," she says. "And I could use some help finding the way." She takes a quick look around. "It's a big place."

It's really astonishing, the size of it; there's just no way of telling from outside. Lena is in a big main corridor, passing doorways with frosted glass and doorways with no glass. Some doors are open and show offices with stacks of files and multiple desks and people very busily going about their business. Phones ring and terminals blink. Every two hundred feet or so, side corridors intersect with the one she's on, and when she looks down one, she sees people walking parallel to her, in rows of multiple main corridors. They're like streets. In fact, every so often there's a small coffee shop or a little sandwich shop. A clothing store as well; even a pharmacy.

Her companion abruptly stops and holds out his hand. "Bossephalus," he says.

She doesn't like his eyes, they're too sharp. She smiles and holds the smile, uncertain about giving him her name.

He winks. "Not to worry," he says. "I'm not the bogeyman."

She un-snares her smile. "Sorry. Sometimes I'm such a New Yorker. My name is Lena."

"Lovely name; I don't hear that often enough. Who are you going to see?"

"Harry Biskabit." It's the only name she knows. Aside, of course, from the supposedly fired Philip Tarrey.

"That's good, that's very good!" Bossephalus chortles. "We both start with B, that'll be easy."

"Of course," she says, trying to sound like this makes perfect sense. They pass a doorway into a large open room

24

with electronic maps displayed along the walls. There are little red beeping lights moving, and people are talking into headsets and clicking on little handheld computers. "Is that what I think it is?" she asks with interest. She has no idea what it is, really, but it seems like a good way to go.

Bossephalus beams and pats her shoulder. "Parking department, downtown unit. Look," he says, pointing as a red light moves closer to a blue light. "Got him!" The blue light disappears and the red moves on. "He thought he had that spot!" Bossephalus claps his hands. "I love that. Drives them crazy upstairs. Parking to kill for! That's what the motto is. I bet that red was driving around for an hour. Those are the ones that are very dear to us."

Lena's mind is racing. The maps on the wall are street maps? They must be street maps. Then the reds are cars looking for parking spots and, if she understands Bossephalus, the blues are parking spots. They disappear in one street and appear in another. There are green lights as well, and the greens always get the spots.

"You're controlling the parking spaces?" she asks. "You're moving your own cars around?"

"That's it! We take the spaces ourselves or sometimes we give them to the luckies. The unluckies *almost* get it, but at the last minute they get stopped by someone crossing the street or a light changes, or a bus blocks the way, and then they can actually see someone else getting the spot they were heading for. Or we put cones up and it suddenly becomes illegal."

"Nice," she says neutrally. "Smooth." She doesn't have a car, doesn't like cars—why would anyone have a car in New York?—but it's not nice, not a bit. What kind of place is this?

Bossephalus taps her on the elbow and they go back into the corridor.

"So you're seeing Biskabit," he says. "Didn't know he was hiring. I could use some help myself. What do you do?"

"Programmer," she tells him. "Strong in html and design."

"Very useful," he says. "We're always looking for web designers. We put a lot of them in startup companies, but now we're branching into corporate."

"The startups didn't do so well," she says cautiously.

"No? We thought it went splendidly."

Splendid? Who could think that all those bankruptcies were a good thing? He must be terribly uninformed. "Where do you work?" Lena asks politely.

He looks at her and smiles. "I'm in Information," he says.

There's something about his smile that's nasty, though she tries to talk herself out of it. Maybe he's just a friendly man showing a newcomer around, she thinks. Maybe.

They come to a wider corridor. She can hear drilling and hammering.

"We're expanding," Bossephalus says, sweeping his hand along the corridor. "Our job keeps getting bigger, and there's a limit to how much we can squeeze into our limited space. So—up we go." He's very cheerful about it.

She squints at the corridor. "Up?"

"They can't have it all," he says easily. "We're willing to put up with a lot, since we like what we do. But as they grow we grow, so we're forced to have some additional entries and vents and a window here and there. Very modest when you consider."

She's trying to piece this together and stupidly repeats, "Up?" Could her downstairs neighbour be on to something? Could they really be taking some of his apartment? It seems incredible, but Bossephalus raises his eyes up to follow his pointing finger. He lifts his chin and the look on his face is satisfied and confident.

"We're really just shifting them around a little. When you think about it, nobody uses all the space they have. Tops of closets, under the sink, behind the tub—add it all together and it's substantial real estate. We have the science to do some adjusting. We're careful not to give them anything concrete to go on."

"I see." She struggles to make her voice noncommittal. "You just make them a little more cramped? When they're already complaining about being cramped?"

He beams. "Nicely put."

They start to pass men on ladders drilling upwards and men with expanders—wide metal brackets with a wheel in the middle—widening the drilled areas. Bossephalus motions for Lena to follow him into a long room with calculators and screens with groups of numbers. "This is one of my favourites," he whispers, and nods towards a lottery machine. "It was my idea to get involved in this. Every third lottery winner will have a problem—we give it to someone who has a warrant out on him, or a guy who'll say it was his own purchase but his buddies at work say it was a group ticket, or a mugger finds the winning ticket in the purse he just stole—that's tricky! What will he do?"

She decides she has to go along with him, cheer along with him. "I like that," she says in an appreciative sort of way. "It's a moral dilemma that's really a legal dilemma. I mean, a criminal dilemma. What to do, what to do." She's trying not to think about implications, any implications. Her mind is snapping around like cut wires.

"You see the fun. Now, I'm getting forgetful. Where am I taking you?" He turns up his smile, it's now bright and gleaming. There's a little edge of intimacy in it, as if he has something up his sleeve.

"Biskabit."

"Oh yes, that's right. And what department is he in?"

"Personnel. Human Resources. Whatever it's called, I forget. They keep changing the name, don't they?"

"Do they?" he says smoothly, as if it doesn't matter to him. "Here's Billings." He waves his arm. "We're sending out cut-off notices to people who have no idea why; we're sending out $10,000 electric bills to small studios; $10,000 phone bills to poor people. The interns make up collection notices with unreadable phone numbers!" He laughs. "We scramble the records at the source, of course."

She thinks of people getting those bills, trying to cope with them. She had a notice from a collection agency once; it drove her crazy. She blurts out, "Why?" She regrets it immediately. Wherever she is—whatever this place is—it's obviously not an ordinary job, these aren't ordinary people. She should keep her head down and shut up.

"Why?" he murmurs, repeating her question in a sad little voice. "When did you hear from Biskabit?"

"I didn't actually hear from him," she says. "I heard

about the job. From a memo. A job description."

"In the papers?" he suggests.

She's blinking too much, she knows she's blinking too much, but she can't stop no matter how much she wants to. "In some papers," she says. "I found some papers."

He sighs. "Come along with me. We're almost there."

They pass more open rooms. Some rooms have signs on them: "Obstruction. Illegal Towing. Merchandise Warranties." One of the biggest rooms says, simply, "Chemicals." She hears people yelling, "Skin reactions! Fumes! No noticeable odour!"

Her feet are getting leaden, she's becoming heavy with dread. If I can just get rid of Bossephalus, she thinks, maybe I can make my way back and out. How many times have we turned? I can't remember how many times we've turned.

"It's a great job," he explains. "You have to love it." He clasps his hands together in delight. "*Love*. It's a chemical, you know. A little bit of a drug in the right place. Sneak it into their coffee or their potato chips—voila! Take it away and forty years of marriage goes down the drain. Of course, sometimes all you have to do is get someone a little sexier, a little more spangled, and put them in the right place. Take someone with the name of Denise, for instance. Smart and sexy and just a little bit dangerous. But you know all about Denise," he says.

Her heart does a little thud. Is this just some wild coincidence, or is Bossephalus talking about the woman who clicked her heels and took her love to Oz?

She passes a screen that shows a massive backup on the bridge. She doesn't look directly; her eyes roll out to the side. The bridge camera swings from the long view to the short view. It's a jackknifed tractor-trailer, as usual. "Why is it always a tractor-trailer?" she asks, trying to make it a joke. "Shouldn't they be outlawed?"

"The Bridge and Tunnel Authority!" he shouts. "We *own* the Bridge and Tunnel Authority! Between that and the construction jobs, we hardly have enough staff. Well, construction doesn't actually need staff once they put up the orange cones, do they?" He's pleased with himself.

Then he puts his hand on her shoulder. At first it's just a slight touch, but he adds weight to it. They turn a corner and there are four people standing there, as if they're waiting.

"The membership committee," Bossephalus says easily. "Come to greet us. You, actually."

There are two men and two women, all in white lab coats. They stand in front of a door marked "Accidents." The women smile at her politely, the men move behind her and she can't see their faces, but she can feel them.

"What's this?" she asks, her mouth dry.

"We've been thinking about what job would be best for you," Bossephalus says. He's very happy.

"Who's 'we'?" She tries to sound tough, but it comes out faintly.

"Think of us as a service organization," he says. "Only we serve ourselves." He points to his ear, which has a small device, like a hearing aid. "I've been getting reports on you all along. Let's go this way." They take a left down another corridor, which has stacks of filing cabinets pushed to one side. "We're digital now, of course," Bossephalus murmurs. "Computers, chips, cameras everywhere. Look it up, nail it down. We keep track of millions of people above us, we visit them, we live among them. And we play a little." He laughs. "We play a lot. We're scientists." His eyes roll toward a sign. "Medical Records." She doesn't like the sign.

"Is this where you work?" Lena asks.

"Me?" He laughs. "No, no, no. You haven't figured it out yet? You can't guess what my job is?" He stops to watch her think.

She looks at the four people who surround them. Each one is looking in a different direction—at the walls, down the corridor, into the rooms that flash with computer screens. "Sometimes I feel that there's a plan," she says finally. "When things go wrong again and again. I keep telling myself it's just bad luck." This isn't the kind of thing she admits. Not normally.

He smiles. "The plan keeps changing," he says agreeably. "Something we do seems good, and we do it; and then someone comes along with a better plan. For the little people," he whispered. "For the pawns. Isn't that how it feels?"

She nods. But she resents it.

"You see, you were never called here. You simply don't belong here. Another accident? Do you think so?" He pats her on the shoulder. She thinks, for a moment, that it's a friendly pat, avuncular.

She can hear names being called out in one of the rooms. Just names, no emotion, then a list of diseases. "Heart attack. Lung cancer. Malaria. Stroke." She steps into the doorway and looks inside. People are standing at whiteboards, where they write and then erase diseases, as if to keep track of trends.

"Food poisoning!" a worker cries. "How about a funeral?"

There's an instant crescendo of agreement. She turns back to Bossephalus. "You're with security, aren't you?"

"Head of," he says cheerily. "Specializing in break-ins. We don't see them too often, we've got a good system of checks and counterchecks. The guards don't look too intelligent, but that's deliberate. If someone is interested, they're going to get in, and it's best if we get them at our own convenience."

"So." She takes a deep breath. "So what happens now?"

He grips her shoulder again and leads her to another room. "It's not so bad," he says in a reassuring tone. "We're going to put you back where you belong. But you won't be in any danger, and neither will we." He waves her forward, over to the main desk in the room. "Shayton," he says. "Lena Shayton."

"Ah," the woman at the desk says. "Got her right here." She turns to the computer screen and starts clicking away.

Lena's hands began to perspire and she feels a lump at the back of her mouth. It's so big she has trouble swallowing. Bossephalus' hand moves up from her shoulder and he spreads his fingers hard around her ear. "Right about here, maybe," he says. "Though I'm not a doctor. But right where the speech centers are, the communication centers."

"Got it!" the desk person calls out. "Here we go!"

"Stop," Lena says. "Fot are ye doon?"

"Not just the sounds," he advises. "Make it the meaning, too."

"Croon wizzes, who saw that blucksbin. Terrible blucksbin!" I try, I try, she thinks.

"That's it!" Bossephalus cries. "That's exactly what I

mean. Give her lots of words without meaning, make it almost make sense."

She can eel her tongue twisting, he says, "Goo." She can't find things, sharp or thin. Is it in her turn? Maybe she can write, with a spit on the knee, so they'll wonder highways and believe then, get a gooseberry rhythm.

Lena Shayton, boom boom, ready now? Upsy upsy.

Whirlybanging all over bingo next Tuesday too. Please please bing she think. Words, she say words.

DOWN ON THE FARM

One of those pigs with the ears all down its back walked by, snorting.

"Little piggy," Tercepia called, bending over and holding her hand out. "Here, here, here."

The pig ignored her.

She was standing next to a crib of grain. She reached in and took a handful and threw it in an arc towards the pig. Some of the ears on its back were moving.

The pig did a little jump and trotted away. Tercepia straightened up and ran after it. The pig went faster and so did Tercepia and all at once she was racing really swiftly, wind in her face and the pig rounded the corner of the barn and she lost sight of it for a moment and that made her run even faster so it wouldn't disappear altogether and she put on a burst.

"No!" Dr. Sandam yelled. He was right there around the corner of the barn. The pig was slowing down, looking back at her, and the doctor's face looked really annoyed. At once she stopped and felt ashamed. She wasn't supposed to chase the pigs. She was never supposed to chase the pigs.

"Pig ran," she said faintly.

"What did I tell you?"

"No chasing pigs," she whispered.

"Only the pigs?"

"No chasing anything."

"And if you do?"

She hung her head. Her hands dangled, her shoulders sank and curved her back. "Sit forever," she said sadly.

"For one hour," he amended. His voice was cheerier, and Tercepia looked up. There was someone else standing next to him and the doctor was looking at this person now, smiling. "An hour seems forever at that age," he was saying. "But the pigs can't be disturbed, of course. Too much agitation and we might damage the implants. Not to mention that the pigs get stressed, and that wouldn't be right."

"Woulda be right," Tercepia agreed, eager to please him.

The doctor's friend looked at her and put a smile on his face, but she didn't trust it. She stepped closer to the doctor, keeping her eyes on the smile.

"This is Portafack," the doctor said. "He wants to look around. Do you want to show him around?"

She hung her head and hid behind the doctor. "Please no. Feed pigs now."

"They're all shy?" Portafack asked. "Or just this one?"

"They like routines," the doctor said and shrugged. "They get nervous when anything changes, and we've had a few changes lately. But yes, the females are a little shyer than the males. Would you prefer a male?"

Portafack's smile went away. "I was interested in the females. Thought they would be . . . well, more docile, I guess. No aggression issues. That kind of thing."

The doctor stepped aside and pulled Tercepia forward. "Yes, there's been a lot of interest in the females. They're smart and submissive, by and large. Here, let me show you what she can do. Tercepia, bring water."

Tercepia looked alert and said "Yes!" eagerly. She was allowed to run to bring water, so she flung herself away. She went back the way she had come, around the corner, and then across the yard to the office, where there was cold water and glasses. She knew how to do that.

That pig was there again, twitching its tail and all its ears, and Tercepia tried very hard not to see it, but when it noticed Tercepia, it did a little pig turnaround and trotted off to the next yard. Tercepia was still in control, but then she saw the dog, which she hadn't seen in hours, and she gave a gleeful little call and ran to the dog, then sat down next to it, and hugged it over and over again.

The dog's mouth moved but there was no sound, so Tercepia kept saying, "Good, good, good Cerbo! Good, good, good dog!" and Cerbo licked her face and then, still silent, looked at her earnestly. He lifted a paw and placed it gently on her knee.

"Food? Water?" Tercepia asked him. She hugged him fiercely and stood up. "Come."

The dog followed her to the office, where she got a bowl of water and put it down for him, and then took sandwiches out of the refrigerator and put them down on the floor.

She sat down and leaned against him for comfort but the dog inched away from her; he was hungry and pulled the sandwiches apart, eating them piece by piece. When he was done he drank the water, which reminded Tercepia of her task. She leaped up and said, "Bring water!" Then she filled two glasses, put them on a tray, and walked out the door, her eyes devoted to the glasses, trying not to walk so fast she would slop them. The dog watched her from the doorway, licking his muzzle fastidiously. When she disappeared, he went over to Portafack's car, lifted his leg, and then walked away in satisfaction.

Tercepia went in search of Sandam and the stranger. They weren't at the first barn, which held more of the pigs with ears. When she was younger she would run in there to pull their ears and the pig would squeal a little and jump and the ears would wiggle. Sandam made her sit still in the middle of all the pigs, sit forever, and she had never done it again, but the ears always made her chin rise up with excitement, and her mouth would open. Even as she passed, she panted a little, longingly, but held the glasses steady and went on to the pens behind the second barn, where the pigs had rows of eyes like polyps growing around their necks like garlands. The eyes rippled as the pigs moved.

"Sometimes they roll over," the doctor was saying, pointing things out to Portafack. "Which the ears can take, but not the eyes. So we made the eyes into a sort of necklace, they suffer less damage that way."

Portafack leaned over to look at a bunch of pigs grunting in a group by the railing. One had brown eyes, about half grown, around its head. It kept twitching.

"Those flies," Portafack said. "Don't they bother the eyes?"

"The eyes are rudimentary at this point," the doctor assured him. "They don't feel a thing. Ah, here she is. You see? Good girl, Tercepia."

She held out the tray, looking around uneasily. She didn't like these pigs. There were hundreds, perhaps thousands, of eyes peering at her from every direction. Her neck prickled; she kept feeling that the eyes were following her. The doctor looked at her steadily as she held the tray.

Portafack was also watching her. "How old is she?"

"Four. The hybrids learn very quickly, though there's a limit. Her vocabulary is about a hundred spoken words, but she understands much more than that. You can teach her. It takes some repetition and reward, but she learns quickly. Her motor skills aren't as good. She can carry things, but nothing too fine. We teach them to pour drinks and to make sandwiches, but we don't allow knives, and no cooking. They can do assembly lines if it's blunt work—nothing like turning screws, for instance. Were you thinking household or assembly lines? They're very good at both, though you have to allow them rest breaks—or exercise breaks, really—after an hour. They make mistakes when they get bored."

"It's incredible. She looks grown up." Portafack's eyes scanned her body. "A little woman," he said.

"Well, for the most part, she is." There was a pause as the men stared at her.

"How long do they live?"

"Our guess is somewhere around 30. They may live longer—after all, they're visibly human; they have human bodies. The dog gene will affect their longevity, of course."

Portafack shook his head. "Dogs," he said. "I had a dog when I was a kid. Broke my heart when I had to destroy him. Those mournful, loving eyes. Hard to think of a world without dogs."

"There's no reason to," Sandam said quickly.

"Does she act like a human girl? Domestic urges, that kind of thing?"

The doctor glanced at Portafack. "You want a household servant, then?"

Portafack's lips twitched slightly. "Yes. I live alone, you see. My life needs a woman's touch." His smile inched across his face again.

"Would you like to see some of the others? You have a choice, you know. After all, if you're going to be seeing her every day, you'd want the one that appeals to your eyes the most, no? I think Tercepia is exceptionally intelligent, but that may be because she was one of the first and I spent a lot of time with her. But there are differences in appearance, too. She does have a slightly more noticeable ridge along the nose; some of the others have less. It's up to you." He turned to lead the way and Portafack glanced at his back for a moment, appraisingly.

Tercepia followed them, away from the eye pigs and past the outside pen with the nose pigs. They headed for a red brick building called The House, which had a front door and windows with curtains.

A pair of young girls answered the doorbell. To Portafack, they looked like they could be twins—or almost twins. There was only a slight difference between them. They wore similar loose dresses and one had a somewhat bigger nose and one had thinner lips

The girls jostled each other and one fell back against a lamp. They lunged together and rolled around the floor.

"Stop!" Sandam shouted, and the girls rolled away from each other, looking slightly shamefaced. "Up!" They got up reluctantly, grabbing each other and bumping in a playful manner.

"Sit," Sandam said, and they began to sit on the floor. "On the sofa," Sandam said, and when they appeared confused, he whispered to Portafack, "They're still in training." Then he walked over to the sofa, called them, and made them sit properly. He saw a certain air of expectation on Portafack's part, so he said, "We never hit them."

"Really? That's remarkable. How do you get them to learn?"

"Repetition and rewards. If they don't do a task right, they don't get a treat. But they want praise, of course. Rewards just tell them they've succeeded."

Portafack raised his eyebrows. "But surely there must be times when they do something wrong? Or when they disobey?"

"We never hit them," Sandam repeated, and Portafack shrugged his shoulders lightly.

They went to the next room, where the larger girls were ironing and washing dishes. One of them was holding a tray with plastic glasses on it. The tray kept sliding forward and the glasses kept dropping.

Tercepia ran up to the girls one by one and just touched them on the arm, and then ran over to another girl. Portafack felt that he could trace the origins of some of the girls quite easily. One had hair that was coarse and slightly mottled. Another had eyes that seemed, to him, to be too close together. Tercepia on the other hand had even features and good hair.

They walked to the porch. The youngest girls were buttoning and unbuttoning their shirts, heads were lowered, their faces frowning in concentration. One girl was biting her lip. "Grooming," Sandam said. "We teach them proper appearance. They don't all reach the same abilities, but we do have some ground rules. They have to bathe and do buttons and zippers. They have to return when they're called. They can't bite." He shrugged. "General rules."

"Biters?" Portafack asked, his eyes traveling slowly over the girls.

"We haven't really had any biters yet. We just try to come up with rules that guarantee hybrids with reliable temperaments."

Sandam followed Portafack's gaze to a girl who was having the most trouble, and whose bare skin was visible. "Perhaps you could give me a little information about yourself?" Sandam asked. "What you're looking for exactly, what kind of household you have. Just in general some background. You mentioned a dog when you were a child. Have you had more pets, children, a wife?"

Portafack drew his eyes away from the girl. "I was married once but divorced. We didn't have children. That was a while ago. I'm very busy and, I'm afraid, rather set in my ways. I like the house to be kept clean and I like simple foods well prepared. I had a housekeeper for many years but she left to get married. That was surprising, she was far too old, I would have thought, to interest anybody. I wouldn't like to lose another one to marriage." He turned back to the girls in front of him. "They don't—well, marry, do they?"

Sandam smiled. "No. Though their sexuality is intact. They might find someone to sleep with occasionally."

"But not get pregnant?" Portafack moistened his lips.

"No. They're sterile. We own the copyright, after all."

"So they don't mind sex," Portafack murmured.

Sandam let the statement rest for a second. "No. We didn't see any reason to take that away. It can enhance their quality of life. You have to remember that they are dominantly human. You have to have some sensitivity, because they do."

"Oh, I'm kind," Portafack said. "No one has ever said I wasn't. They do prepare food, I see?" He was watching as the girls made sandwiches.

"Meals are really pretty simple. They don't have much of an attention span so we've given up on using a stove. They forget about it and walk away. You might as well tell me exactly what your requirements are. Cleaning, simple meals?"

"Laundry, ironing. Can they do shopping?"

"Simple things only, I'm afraid. They don't read."

"Oh?" Portafack considered this. "I'm surprised. Is that deliberate?"

"No, we've tried teaching them. Their intellectual capacity varies from one to the other, but the best comprehends about as much as a 6 year old. They can be extremely sensitive, and unable to express it well."

"She looks ..." Portafack began. "Her name is Tercepia, right? She looks like a normal girl. A normal young girl." His voice was soothing. He was looking at Tercepia more and more as she helped a friend make sandwiches. She wrapped two and put them in her pocket.

"We spent a lot of time with her. Of course she was one of the first group."

"Oh? And what happened to the others?"

Sandam hesitated briefly. "It was just her and two males. We had trouble with one of them and he's not for release. We keep him separated from the others, since he's not really trainable. We can generally tell from their appearance how well they'll do."

"I suppose the ones who look too much like a dog get sent to the pound?" Portafack joked.

Sandam's face froze and eyes shifted to the window. Then he produced a short laugh and said, "Nothing that drastic, I assure you. It's very rare. Most of the hybrids are running the way we want now."

"Oh, that's right," Portafack said. "They're born in a group, aren't they? Multiple births. I suppose you don't call them a litter, do you?" He laughed and Sandam dutifully laughed with him. "Are the mothers the humans? How does that work?"

"We use cow surrogates, of course."

"Cow surrogates." Portafack shook his head. "I've heard of that. I thought it was for women who didn't want to ruin their figures. But I guess you can mix anything in a test tube and stick it in a cow these days?"

"Well, that's pretty simplified. We actually use gene-splicing; we can manipulate DNA, so we mix and match genes. We still have a lot to learn, but we're getting there. We change things a little for each generation." He gestured lightly towards the girls, with their differences in doglike facial appearances. "We hope to get to the point where we can produce hybrids for assembly lines, for care-taking positions, for general manual labour, and we're looking into exhibition sports as well. They can run fast and catch things, so it seems a possibility. But I'm happy with girls like Tercepia. She's really got the best of both breeds—eager and loving like a dog but looking very human. The other male in her group has turned out very well. He was one of the three hybrids we placed last week, and we've already gotten good reports on him. Like Tercepia, he's exceptional, though a little more outgoing. There's another boy now that looks promising. Smart and strong."

"No," Portafack mused, "I don't want a boy. I like Tercepia."

"Then let me suggest this. Why don't you try talking to her and seeing how she responds? I can send her over to the eggs. She loves those. When you get there, pick up one of the eggs that's about to hatch—look for a slight crack in the shell. It will get her interest. Then you can walk around with her and see how it goes."

"It's a little bit like a date," Portafack joked.

"A trial."

"A test run. That's fine by me. How do I get her to come?"

She was over by the sink, running water and filling glasses. She would occasionally duck her head in the jet of water and drink.

"Tercepia," Sandam called.

She wiped her mouth and came over to him.

"Go to the eggs," he said. "Bring me an egg."

"Egg," Tercepia repeated in a happy voice. She turned and began to skip out the door.

"You'd better hurry if you're going with her. They're always in a rush."

Portafack almost lunged in his haste, and he was forced to trot briefly in order to keep her in sight. She went off to the left and around the back of the barns, stopping briefly to run over to a brown dog that was circling a tree. The dog turned once to look at Portafack, and he got a look at its eyes. They surprised him. They were blue, and unlike most dogs' eyes, they had a pronounced white rim. Startlingly human-looking, he thought, and he didn't like it. The blue-eyed dog studied him for an instant, but Tercepia pushed it in fun and the two of them began to run together along the sides of the barn. They took turns chasing each other and otherwise wasting time, or Portafack would have lost them.

They stopped and the girl bent down and hugged the dog.

"Tercepia!" Portafack yelled sharply. She jerked up and looked at him. "Egg!" he called.

The blue-eyed dog laid its ears flat against his head and trotted off to the trees, the edge of a woodlands that began a few hundred yards from the pens. Tercepia's gaze followed him.

"Egg!" Portafack repeated to get her attention again. She turned and walked ahead of him.

Portafack passed an opening in the barn and saw pigs inside with rows of noses along their spine. He made a face. A few more yards and Tercepia turned into a small building.

There were elevated glassed-in terrariums with heat lamps along one wall. Across from them were chickens in large cages. At the far end there was laboratory equipment and a few technicians. One got off the phone and waved at Portafack. He pointed to the glass cage where Tercepia was standing, so he went over and selected an egg with a pronounced crack.

He held it in his palm. It was warm and heavy and he covered it with his fist for a moment, just testing its weight. He felt a vibration in the egg, a kind of internal wiggle.

"Look, Tercepia," he said. "I think it's hatching."

Tercepia grinned and stuck her head over the egg, blocking his view. He could smell her slightly, a little grubby, a little salty. He took a slow breath and moved his hand higher, luring her closer.

She brushed against him, intent on the egg. It was moving gently from side to side and he could feel a sort of thump now. He moved the egg from one hand to the other, and Tercepia followed it so she was no longer beside him but in front of him. Her eyes were stuck on the egg. He took his free hand and brushed it against her arm in a studied, casual way. He was watching her even as he felt the egg move. He had to control his breathing so she wouldn't notice anything. His fingertips moved gently forward. She was wearing a thin cotton dress. It wasn't fresh. She had been wearing it long enough so that it had softened and lay against her skin. His fingers touched the side of her breast. It would seem like an accident. He could smell her hair.

She moved slightly when he touched her, shifting her weight differently, but her head blocked his view of the egg. He was more interested in accidentally touching her again, to see what her reaction would be. But then the egg began to thump in the palm of his hand and a very natural curiosity caused him to push her slightly aside so he could see.

The thumping, or whatever it was, was rocking the egg noticeably. He listened for little pecks or some kind of chirping; he was sure that would happen as soon as the shell was broken, but it didn't exactly break. Instead, the egg seemed to bulge a little at one point, and the rocking took on a strong rhythm. The bulge was noticeable.

Suddenly the shell broke, and a dark pink thing poked out. It was soft and thick and curled a little like a tube.

Portafack was fascinated and repulsed. He felt Tercepia trembling with excitement.

The pink thing poked out some more and the shell broke in half.

"It's a tongue," he said, finally recognizing it, and Tercepia lunged forward, pushing her head in again over the egg. He thought she might eat it, so he grabbed her by the upper arm, holding her tightly. She twisted away, but her eyes were still trained on the egg. He held it out slightly, liking the way she struggled against him.

The tongue wiggled against his palm. He dropped it in surprise and the girl tried to fall down on top of it. She crouched low and he bent down. "No," he said. "Don't eat it. No."

The second "no" caused her to move back on her haunches, her eyes still trained on the egg, which was wriggling on the ground. He didn't want to touch it, so he looked around, back over the lab area, and called out, "This one's hatched and I think she might eat it."

A man in a lab coat hurried over and picked up the tongue.

"Stay," Portafack said when she started to follow the technician. She stopped and looked at him. "Good. That's very good. Come here now." She went to him, reluctantly.

He lifted her chin with his hand, studying her. The girl's face had a slight ridge from her forehead to her nose. It was hard for him to figure out whether she looked dull-witted or smart, because it all depended on perspective, didn't it? From whose point of view, human or dog? "Are you a good girl?" he breathed into her face.

"Or do you fight back? Which will it be?" His voice was coaxing; Tercepia tensed and he released her.

"Let's go to Dr. Sandam, shall we?" he said. She looked alert, and he repeated, "Sandam." She took off at a trot.

He didn't take much notice of the brown dog that was in sight again, moving through the trees a hundred yards from the barn. Tercepia saw the dog and started running to him, but Portafack called her back and she moved in an arc on line again to go find Sandam.

He watched her run. She was barefoot, with strong calf muscles. Her arms pumped rhythmically. He would let her hair grow longer; right now it was short and uncared for. He didn't mind its roughness, but he wanted it to get in her face more; he wanted to be able to twist it around in his hand.

Sandam was standing outside, waiting for them.

"Well?" he asked.

"I'll take her," Portafack said. "If she's as good as you say, I'll probably come back and take some more. I have friends who will be interested."

Sandam nodded. "I have to admit I'm sorry to see her go. She's very sweet and very loyal. She may seem depressed for a few days, they do sometimes, until she adjusts. We spent a lot of time on her." There was regret in his voice as he led Portafack to his office and began writing out the receipts. "It was a pleasure to see how much she could learn. I do want you to send me reports every month or so. We want to track them as much as possible. Her brother's reports have been good, and we sold two of the younger girls last week as nannies. They've adjusted very quickly, though the first few days, I have to warn you, can be very sad for them."

When he had finished all the paperwork, he handed the bill to Portafack, who studied it and then gave him a credit card.

"How will she know she belongs to me now?"

"She's trained to accept orders, so use voice commands, just as you would with any dog. But be kind. They respond to kindness more than anything else. Persuasion. Affection. That sort of thing."

When they'd finished all the paper work, they went outside again. Tercepia was playing with the dog a little distance away.

"That dog," Portafack murmured. He could see the dog opening and shutting its mouth, but there was no sound. "Did you de-bark it or something?"

Sandam cleared his throat. "It made too much noise. It kept distracting the hybrids."

"Oh? Then barking bothers them?"

Sandam hesitated. "No. It wasn't really the barking that did it, but don't worry. It doesn't affect you."

"If you say so. Do I just call her to me?" He was eager; his eyes were locked on her.

He called and the girl came to him, but stood a few feet away. She looked uneasy. The blue-eyed dog went off to the other side of the yard, and sat down watching them.

"Car, Tercepia," Sandam said. He patted Portafack on the shoulder. "She likes cars. They all do."

"I could have guessed. Let's go to the car, Tercepia."

Tercepia looked alert when she heard the word and happily ran over to Sandam's car.

"No," he said.

"Here, Tercepia," Portafack said, motioning her to the

right vehicle. "Car." He opened the door for her.

She went over slowly and climbed in. When Portafack closed the door, she looked alarmed and stared at Sandam. She began to whimper.

"Don't worry about that," Sandam said as he walked Portafack to the driver's side. "She'll be upset for a day or two then she'll settle down."

"Still, I hope she doesn't make a lot of noise," Portafack said. "It's annoying."

"Give her some treats if she doesn't eat. But no chocolate, they can't tolerate it, a legacy of the dog genes."

Portafack laughed. "Flowers? Should I get flowers?"

"She likes cheese. Goodbye, Tercepia. Be good." Sandam waved as Portafack started the motor.

The long driveway curved at one point, and they lost sight of the farm. It was at that moment that Tercepia began to howl. She shoved herself against the seat belt, rocking as close to the windshield, seat, or window as she could as the car moved. She tried desperately to get back to Sandam.

"Stop it," Portafack said. "Sit. Sit!" He jerked his foot on the accelerator, then stepped on the brakes so he could pull her back, then accelerated again, only to stop as her arms windmilled wildly. She began to howl, "Home, home home!" in a drawn out high voice. She clutched at the seat belt, holding it tight or pulling it away from her chest. "Home, home, home!" she wailed.

Portafack had to slow down; it was hard to drive with Tercepia's constant movements. The brown dog suddenly appeared in the road in front of him, barking soundlessly, and then the dog ran to the passenger side of the car. It leapt in the air and threw itself against Tercepia's door.

"Cerbo!" Tercepia cried out, and her hands pumped at the side window. "Cerbo, help! Cerbo, home, home! Please Cerbo. Tercepia sorry! Home now, home now!" She wept openly, then twisted around in the seat to smack Portafack. She howled at him, hitting wildly, snapping at his arm, pulling at his face, his nose, his ears, anything she could lay hands on. Portafack couldn't see. He stopped the car and jerked it in park, snapping Tercepia forward. This caught her by surprise, so he took the opportunity to grab her by the arm and smack her head. His face twisted at her, his mouth ugly, his voice harsh as he shouted, "I'll beat the crap out of you if you don't stop!" He unlocked his seat belt to have better aim.

A huge rock crashed into his windshield.

He was startled and let Tercepia's arm go. What had fallen on them?

It wasn't a rock; it was that dog again and it was hurling itself again at the windshield, fangs bared, tongue curled, ears pricked high and those eerie blue eyes staring at him with a ferocious concentration that made his hands sweat.

He blasted the horn. If it didn't frighten the dog, maybe it would bring Sandam. He felt trapped.

Tercepia's hands flailed at his face, scratching, poking, ramming a fist into his right eye. She was mindless, a maniac, frantic; her weird shrieking combining with the sounds of the dog's claws on the side of the car incapacitated him.

Tercepia unlocked the door and bolted.

Cerbo broke free and began to run up to the trees that ringed the farm. She ran after him. In the distance, up the drive, she could see Sandam's hurrying figure and she heard his voice floating towards her. "Tercepia! Here! Now! Here! Come here!" but she ignored it.

She stopped on the ridge, catching her breath. She sat down so she could hug the dog even more. Cerbo licked her face, her hands, his muzzle moving constantly.

Cerbo lifted his head and his ears twitched. Tercepia turned to see where he was looking, and there was Portafack, with a heavy stick in his hand and a length of rope. "Get over here, girl," he said. "Get over here or I'll kill the two of you. You're going to have to learn to listen to me now."

Tercepia leaped up, spun around, and began to run through the woods, Cerbo running beside her. Portafack stayed halfway up the hill, running after her, panting loudly. They came out of the trees, and Portafack could see some buildings in the distance—he thought they were the schools. To the left was a fenced-in field with cows in it, and Tercepia seemed to be going straight for it.

The cows were standing as if watching them, face forward. They had projections from their sides and when he got closer, Portafack saw that they were rudimentary arms. The arms were bare and of slightly different lengths. The fingers moved in the air like they were rolling balls or playing piano, constantly moving. He felt an instant's revulsion, but his fury led him forward. He saw Tercepia and the dog run to the middle of the cows and stop. Tercepia was pointing at him and crying.

He was surprised that the two of them had stopped. He thought he might have outrun them, somehow, might have outmaneuvered them. Perhaps, like some animals that hid a part of themselves they thought he couldn't see them. But he could, and he was going to teach them a lesson.

He waved his stick, but then he thought better of it. He didn't want a struggle, he wanted to get close to her and tie her hands up. If he looked frightening, she might run again. He held the stick behind his back with his right hand.

"Here, Tercepia," he called sweetly. "It's okay. Good girl. Come here. Don't worry. It's all right."

The cows were shifting and moaning. He pushed the head of one cow out of his way.

The dog came racing at him and he lifted the stick and whacked him on the side. It jerked away with its mouth open but still silent, stumbling a few times, its head down. The cow next to him mooed loudly and the arms along its side began to wave. Portafack stepped away from it. He couldn't see what was behind him. He stepped back from one cow only to find himself between two others. He lifted his stick again, automatically, as arms reached for him, and in an instant the noise in the field rose. The cows moaned angrily and surrounded Portafack. He lifted the stick and began to swing blindly, as arms came at him from all sides.

He went down among the hooves endlessly moving around him, catching fragmented glimpses of the girl and the dog seen through the motion of the cows' legs, the oncoming crush of their low stomachs, the jabbing torment of those arms tightening around his throat and covering his face.

"Tercepia!" Sandam called, coming closer, but he was too far away, too far away; the weight of the cows came at Portafack and the hands pressed forward, reaching at him, finding him.

"Home, home, home," Tercepia cried and danced with the dog. She held its front paws and they pranced around together, the dog on its back legs, its blue eyes trained on her. "Happy now," Tercepia said. "Happy here forever. Cerbo, happy with you!"

The blue-eyed dog raised its head and moved its mouth. Portafack's eyes were closing, it was his last sight as a cow stepped on him and the hands held him down.

"Brother!" Tercepia cried again. "Brother forever!"

THE GREAT SPIN

"Well, there's gonna be a Rapture. All the sanctified people will be called to God. They'll leave the Earth. Called to God." Jonah made helpful gestures, his chin upturned, his eyes to the sky, his arms whooshing up.

"What will happen to the goods?" his friend Joey asked, interested.

Jonah frowned. "The Good?"

"The stuff. Will the cars and TVs go up too, or will they stay here?"

"That's not important."

"It is to me," Joey said excitedly. "I'm stayin' behind. I'll make a killin'. I bet I could get a good deal on a house, too. Not this shit we're livin' in now."

"Now, wait," Jonah said, slightly annoyed. "That's the wrong way of looking. You should want to *go* . . ."

"The bank accounts too," Joey said, excited. "Can you put my name on your account, you know, leave it in *trust*. Get your Church to all, like, leave it in *trust* for me? I could water your lawns or whatever. Services rendered."

Jonah sighed. "You're missing the point."

Joey smacked him on the back. "The point is, you're

good and I'm not. I get it. You spend a lot of time at Church, I'm watchin' TV. You sing hymns, I like Rap. Rap, Rapture, I wonder if there's a connection." He snapped his fingers, both hands, and shook his head.

Jonah tried to pity him, because he knew he *should* pity him, because his parents would *tell* him to pity Joey for his sinful fate. But Jonah liked Joey too much to visualize his damnation. Instead Jonah saw—in full Panavision—Joey sauntering around in left-behind clothes and a good car, grinning like a lottery winner. Having fun. Always having fun.

Joey whistled—not a tune, but a series of random notes; he was always doing that. He pulled out notes like a man jingling change. The world would certainly be different after this Rapture, he thought. He liked Jonah and certainly would miss him, but it would be interesting to see who disappeared and who would be left behind with him. It would be fun to see them disappear, actually.

"Huh," he said. "How do you do it? I mean, does everyone float up all at once or is it alphabetical or by age? I bet it'll be on TV. So how does it work?"

Jonah shrugged. "We all float up together. Or we all just disappear while the rest of you blink. There's an argument about it."

Joey bit his lower lip thoughtfully. "We don't all blink at the same time."

"But you *could*," Jonah said.

Joey admitted they could. "Of course I could get a camera and watch you. Or you know," he got excited, "I could put a camera *on* you so I could see you lookin' down at me as you floated away. Because you know when it's gonna happen, right?"

"A week from today," Jonah said.

"And the time?"

"Sunset-ish. Seven PM."

"Good," Joey nodded. "I don't want to miss prime time. I like my TV."

Jonah sat with his family in the yard. They had all showered and put on their best clothes. His little sister, Gina, clutched her favourite doll. Joey had not shown up, and Jonah was relieved. And the weather was still good. They had gone through storms all week, dry storms with high winds. Another front had been predicted, but hadn't shown up. They felt blessed.

His father led them in prayers and then they sang together, and then his father read to them from Thessalonians. The birds put up a mighty ruckus, and when his family sang it seemed to Jonah that the birds joined in, shouting the joy of God in their bird way.

Jonah kind of liked it. It did seem like the attention of the universe was focused on him. On them. A breeze came through, like an angel's wings, and he could feel the presence of God. His parents and his church were always talking about the presence of God and up till then he hadn't been quite sure about it, though he learned to drop his voice to a whisper and smile with encouragement whenever it was discussed.

But now he felt it, like a splendid sunset hitting his chest. And it *was* a splendid sunset, right on cue, with blues and pinks and purples. Clouds chugged along the horizon, picking up colours and getting bigger. Gathering. As he had already noticed, the birds sang like they were convinced of something.

Finally they all held hands on the last "Amen" and lowered their heads and waited, their eyes closed. God, he knew, would breathe in, and they would rise on His breath.

The first few moments were calm and steady, but nothing happened. Time went on, the birds got still, the wind picked up, and Jonah peeked out through his lids. His mother's face was lifted up to the sky, her lips faintly parted and Jonah could tell she was breathing through her mouth. Gina was wide-eyed, looking around in the evening. Her hand had already abandoned Jonah's hand, but she still held on to her father, who had a frown line appearing now just above his brow. A frown or a shadow—it was rapidly getting dark. And then there was a loud crack—this was it!—and the heavens opened and a rain came down like a booby trap. They stood up slowly and went inside.

The next morning Jonah's parents were very quiet. They never listened to the radio or the TV for news in the morning, just said their prayers and ate their breakfast. That morning was dreary.

"Maybe we got the calculations wrong," his father said. "They were very delicate." He looked better than his wife, who seemed to be huddling even as she prepared breakfast. The rapt look she'd had was gone, replaced by uncertainty.

"The numbers were checked," she said softly. "Over and over. We've been waiting for years."

Jonah's parents, of course, disliked Joey but he hadn't actually been forbidden to see him. Instead, a sentence would pop up in their talk every so often. "I hear that

Joey is failing in math. Does he need a tutor?" or "See if Joey can make it to Bible study this week. If he's a friend, save his soul."

Joey's soul seemed pretty sturdy, and he went to Bible study only once, where he smiled gamely and asked confusing questions. He said, for instance, that the bible wasn't meant to be literal. He said he'd been told that by an ex-nun and a Reformed rabbi. The rabbi had impressed him. "He's *reformed*," he repeated. "Gone straight."

"I'm not sure your friend is the right friend to have," Jonah's father said.

"And he may be bad for you; he may accept sinful situations and make them seem harmless to you," his mother added. "Out of ignorance. Because he doesn't know any better."

"He doesn't have God," his father confirmed. "And when you don't have God you're condemned to Hell. You know that."

The fact that Joey was going to Hell made it harder than ever for Jonah to give him up. The rules his parents laid out were clear: he should be polite to Joey, but he should ignore him whenever possible. But Joey was always interesting; Jonah felt his own life was boring, and predetermined. He was at that age when he wanted to be surprised, to be alerted, and maybe even to stun someone in return. He was thinking about the last conversation they'd had, when the Rapture was imminent and Joey was going over all the things he might pick up cheap.

"Now look at that," he'd said, nudging with his chin as he looked out the school bus. "That would be good to have, a dog like that. If you guys take off, let me know where the dogs are so I can pick one out."

Jonah looked and saw a big dog sitting in front of its dog house.

"I'm thinkin' about a career with dogs," Joey continued. "Maybe search-and-rescue, or trainin' them. I like it when they do what they're told, you know? Even when they're not exactly *told*—when you click or make a noise or raise your arm and they jump."

"Like an airplane," Jonah said. "Remote control."

Joey nodded, once. "And what about you? You still goin' into space?"

It sounded sarcastic, at first, since they were going to ascend soon, but Jonah had once said he wanted to be an astronaut. That was before the date had been announced. He always loved to look at the sky. It was mixed up with God, of course; he wanted to see with God's eye: the earth compact below, the stars around him like hair. He didn't know if Joey experienced this same surge of goodness, of wanting to bless and be blessed coming from all his skin, all the cavities of his body. Joey talked about sex all the time, of course, as if that was similar for him. Jonah had been excused from Sex-Ed classes on religious grounds and he got all his information from Joey now. Most often it was crude and boasting, but Joey included masturbation in his talk, and it was the only time Jonah heard about it or sex without the smack of shame.

"That girl," Joey breathed, as one of the other buses drew beside them, and a fully-formed girl in a pullover raised her eyebrows and stared. "That girl."

But Jonah didn't want to hear. "About the dogs," he said. "Why don't you get a dog?"

"I have a dog already," Joey said. "But it's old and small. Doesn't do anythin'. I can get another dog when I get a job, but if I get a job while I'm in school I won't have time for a new dog. One of my dad's tricks."

The bus with that girl pulled ahead of them as they neared school and for a while Joey pretended they were in pursuit, chasing her.

"There are girls in heaven," Jonah said.

Joey shrugged. "But no sex. Never heard of any screwin' up there." He snorted. "*Heaven*. Right."

Jonah's face lit up. "Souls meet," he said. "They meet and touch. It's like telepathy, almost, how you don't need the body—"

"The body's the *point*," Joey said in disgust.

"No, no, no," Jonah reassured him. "There's love. Love is more than the body, isn't it? You love your mother, you love your father—"

"Not that much. Not that way."

"All right, you love a girl. You love her a whole lot, but she won't sleep with you. Do you stop loving her?"

"Yes," Joey said strongly. He twitched all over, happy with himself.

Jonah was trying to think of a way to reach his friend. He knew that everything Joey had just said was a sin, just as everything Joey did was a sin, and everything Joey thought, probably, was a sin. But he believed he could save Joey's soul, and he thought it was worth saving.

"How do you think about God so much?" Joey asked. "I mean, where do you go with it? It's like thinkin' of the colour red. You get it in your mind and then that's it."

"No. When I go on thinking about it, I see the sky and it expands and the stars blink and I keep watching. I think of God and the whole world expands and I feel ready to burst."

Joey laughed meanly. "And you call that God, that burstin' feeling?"

Jonah's face felt hot. "I know what you mean and that's not it. I know what you're talking about and it's completely different."

"Oh sure, sure," Joey said. "I must have a lot of God in me, 'cause I'm burstin' all the time. With holy love," he said, pleased with himself. "Burstin' with holy love."

Jonah felt a sharp loneliness at the way Joey was mocking him. He believed there was a strong bond between them, but it was always slipping away, and then coming back, and then slipping away.

The morning after Rapture, Joey wasn't on the school bus, which was filled with kids whispering and crying. Jonah found a seat by himself, avoiding everyone. He suspected they all knew the Rapture hadn't come, that they were whispering about him.

But the whispering and crying were all over the schoolyard. Finally, he just stood and looked around. No one was pointing at him or laughing at him. It all began to register, finally: something was wrong.

He passed two sobbing girls, four stiff-shouldered boys. One of the very youngest students stood all by himself, wailing, his arms stiffly at his side.

He saw Corinne, who sat next to him in homeroom.

"Didn't anyone tell you?" she asked, blinking. "That storm last night. There was a tornado. It got the bus over on that hilly road to Bightsville. They were coming back from a game. Didn't you notice that storm? It was terrible."

"It was just some rain," Jonah said, arguing. "I know

because I was outside when it happened." Then he was struck, both by the look of contempt in Corinne's eyes and by his own thoughts. He was beginning to worry. "What happened?"

"A lot of people died—that's what happened." It was almost as if she hated him, as if she thought he had something to do with it.

"Who died?" he whispered.

She began to name off all the boys and girls. He knew some of them. He was relieved every time he heard a name he didn't recognize; every time the name wasn't his friend Joey.

"Joey," she finally said. She glared at him.

"What?" he said, jumping back slightly. "Joey?"

She nodded, and wiped her eyes. "The whole bus," she said. "Every single one of them. All gone."

Jonah walked away from her. His head had gotten a little dull; he kept thinking that sometimes Joey hitched a ride home and he didn't usually do after-school stuff. Sure, once he showed up at band practice as a goof, but all he'd done was cause trouble. And he'd only gone to one or two games before. Why would he go when he knew the Rapture was coming?

Maybe Corinne had it wrong. She was a smart kid, but she only knew what she'd heard.

He lifted up his head, then, and scanned the crowds. It was the same kids in the same groups everywhere. They held to their regular spots.

Tommy came up to him and said, "Bummer, no? Joey?" And he shook his head and put his hands in his pockets and went off.

The teachers were gesturing for everyone to come in;

a few of them were even going around to the groups, putting their hands on arbitrary shoulders, leading them. Jonah got caught in front of a group and had to go forward, into school. They were led into the assembly.

The buzz of words got quieter. Kids filed in and sat down, their eyes scanning the room.

The principal started telling them how sorry he was, and that there were grief counsellors to help all of them deal with this tragedy. And he listed the names of all the dead, no—the "known dead." There were two bodies not yet identified, and of course, there were two students unaccounted for. Results were awaited.

He included Joey when he read off the names of the dead. But Joey was capable of bad jokes, of bad taste, of not knowing when to respect other people's feelings. Joey was capable of fudging this somehow.

However: "accounted for and identified." Could Joey really pull that off?

He stood in line for the grief counsellors. "I don't think Joey's really dead," he said.

The counsellor smiled sadly, then consulted a list. "He really is," she said. "What you're feeling is very natural, it's called denial. The first thing you do is insist that the facts are wrong. Because you can't, at first, accept it. It's a terrible thing, it really is, but it happened."

Jonah sat there, miserable and polite. Joey was dead.

There was a half-day at school. He went home and sat in the kitchen. So, apparently his parents hadn't heard or they would be there, waiting for him. Wouldn't they?

He sat at the kitchen table, his head feeling very heavy, and he thought about it. He could find no way to put all this together. He wondered, shamefully, if Joey had left him anything. He was always going on about how Jonah should turn his stuff over because of the Rapture.

I bet he didn't see this coming, Jonah thought. I bet he was really surprised. It was supposed to be me.

When his mother got home, Jonah said, "Joey ascended."

"No," she said. "I understand what you're feeling. It's a shock. We were all prepared for ourselves, and it's a disappointment, but one thing has nothing to do with the other thing."

"It happened at sunset."

"Coincidence."

"You always say there is no coincidence with the Lord."

"I think you should pray harder. As soon as your father comes home, we'll pray. You'll feel better. We'll pray for Joey's soul." She looked away a little at that.

"You think he's burning in Hell!" Jonah said, suddenly understanding that look.

His mother sighed. "Of course he is," she said gently. "You know that too."

His father was depressed. "The numbers all added up to this," he said. "And we invited the Lord into our hearts and lived for Him. Does it make sense to you that He would abandon us like that?"

His father had been born with the name Robert, but he took the name Paul when he converted, because he was struck suddenly, mid-life, mid-path, by the Lord. He'd been on a walk in the park and stumbled on a church picnic, and there, standing as if waiting for him, in a ray of sunlight, was Ann Mary. "Come along now," she'd said gently, turning, "he's about to speak." And this was how he entered the Church of Rising Saints, and how he was persuaded that the Rapture's date was revealed in the Bible, if you read carefully and did your math. From that point on, his life had felt luminous and populated. The Rapture had been far enough in the future not to seem frightening then, and over the years he had learned to accept it hungrily—all of them, together, glorious.

Ann Mary worked for the Church for a very low wage, doing clerical matters and filing various forms. Paul, however, worked in the world, delivering packages for a shipping company. He was friendly to his coworkers and had, once only, and a long time ago, tried to give out pamphlets from his Church. Now he tried to smile, be gentle, never foul-mouthed, be polite—he tried to live as an emblem of his religion and not mix. Not be polluted. Over the years, he had invited a co-worker or two to his home, but it had always been disappointing. They had come in eagerly, and left even more eagerly. They did not want to discuss God; no one in that world wanted to discuss God.

And God was the background sound in Paul's life: the resonance, the resource, the high-pitched whine.

Each day he went out to *their* world, each night he came back to his own. In love with God, with Church, with Ann Mary. His wife believed her children went fortified out to the heathens, flowing in the safety of their belief. She had been out there—knew that it was possible to love the endearments of the damned; it was hard not to wish they could be saved, but she had learned that for all their humour and ease, they could line up against you.

So Jonah kept a sort of cautious silence about his life, and was solitary at school, until Joey sought him out.

Joey looked poor and unkempt; he had a nervous energy and a compulsion to pursue his own curiosity. He heard, once, that Jonah belonged to a cult, and he attached himself to Jonah like a dog.

"We are not a cult," Jonah's father said stiffly. "Cults do not praise the Lord, they praise the leader of the cult. They're heresies." He paused, took a breath, and said, "Everywhere you go, people believe in someone or something—God. Everyone has a version of God. But they're not all true. They represent how much people can or will understand. In a way, it's like music. Some people like classical, some folk, some rock. Music speaks to people, yet there are higher and lower forms of music. So why do some people love the low forms of music? Because it's all they can understand. It's how far they've gone with their abilities—with their souls."

"But why wouldn't God give everyone the higher soul?"

"He does; they choose what to do with it."

"Why can't they all be saved?" Jonah cried.

"They don't want it."

Jonah stopped. He knew there was no use in arguing, that everything he said would float out alone to be swatted by his father's voice. He could never feel his own conviction; he seemed too new at it. But his parents' faith seemed so sure. He regretted it, that he would leave Joey behind, but it had also, in a strange way, seemed obvious. Joey wasn't like them. He wasn't like Joey.

"What if the date was right?" Jonah whispered. He could see his father's mouth twist. "And we weren't the ones who were called?"

Jonah went to Joey's house to see if Joey really did have a dog. He felt responsible for it, because of the way Joey had talked about the left-behind dogs.

Mrs. Pattimpot answered the door, red-eyed, exhausted. "You can't have his dog. What did you say your name was? Oh, yes, he talked about you." She looked away above the trees, then her glance came down again. "I don't know about a pact. I don't know." She didn't seem to be deciding anything. "I don't know. For a while, okay. Just leave me your address and phone number."

She stepped back, opening the door. Behind him, its tail tucked, its ears flat, was a little gray dog. Kind of curly-haired; mournful, shivery.

He bent down and picked it up.

"Wait!" Mrs. Pattimpot said, and went deep inside the house. She came back with a plastic shopping bag. "Buster's dog food," she said, handing it to Jonah.

She closed the door as soon as he stepped outside. Jonah looked in the bag and found a leash. He clipped it onto Buster's collar, and talked to the dog in a soothing tone. "It's perfectly all right. Joey is the one who told me all about you, so nothing bad will happen. You won't be alone," he said firmly. "We're going to rescue all of them." He stopped and took a sheet of paper from his pocket. His lips moved as he read the next address. There was an old Labrador in the yard there who looked at him hopefully. "Shane," he said, "come along, Shane." He went to Matt's house and collected Sophie, then to Sandy's and got the two Chichuahuas, Lefty and Righty.

The dogs sniffed each other, wagged their tails, showed their teeth, but none of them fought. The males took their turns lifting their legs on a post or a tree, and they would have done it endlessly, one after the other, if Jonah hadn't grown tired of it.

He took the dogs home, locked them in his room, and went out for the rest. When his parents came home, they paused outside their door, listening to the yapping. There was a note on the door: *Don't come in yet. Dogs loose—Jonah*.

They knocked, and Jonah opened a window and leaned out. The wild yapping was louder. "I'm sorry," he said. "But you'll have to go somewhere else for a while, just till I figure it out. The house is filled with dogs. There's no more room."

"Jonah—" his father said sternly.

"The problem is, they're excited. I think they'd bite if anyone else came in. They're sorting themselves out—you know, hierarchy. They're finding their hierarchy. Could you give me a few hours?"

His parents stood there, listening. Ann Mary squeezed Paul's hand. "Jonah, are you safe in there?"

"Oh, I'm safe, sure. They like me. I just think they need to settle down a little." He bent down and disappeared for a moment. When he popped up again, he had Buster in his arms. "This is Joey's dog." He flushed a little. "I said I'd take care of him. The other dogs belonged to the rest of the kids who died."

His parents were silent for a while. "All right," his father finally sighed. "But you have to get them in order. Put them in the yard or downstairs or something. They can't be everywhere. And you have to give them back eventually, you know. They're not yours."

The Reverend's house was in an uproar. Church members came and went, grouped on the porch or in the living room, in the back yard. Half the congregation thought the Rapture had taken place without them; half thought their math was wrong, or they had used the wrong calendar. Quite possibly calendars themselves were artificial counting tools.

"It's the nature of inspiration," one member was heatedly saying, "to have *specific* meanings, not universal meanings, so the predictions might apply to some, not all."

"Of course, no one argues with that, but *we're* the *some*. We're the ones."

"Do you even *hear* your lack of humility? Can you wonder why you were left behind?"

"Not left behind—just waiting a little longer—unlike some people who think you either flip the card or don't flip the card in the universe—"

"Now what that means I don't even think *you* can explain—"

Paul and Ann Mary and Gina stood in the backyard, listening to the arguments around them. Ann Mary slipped her hand inside her husband's hand. They had hoped to talk to the Reverend about Jonah and the dogs.

"There was a transposition," someone argued. "The commonest mistakes. Nine years from now—"

"Or nine years *ago*—or nine days, or nine hours *ago*—if it's a mistake, who says it's in favour of the future?"

"Because *we're still here*," an exasperated voice cried, and the debate raged on.

"This is no good," Ann Mary said finally.

Paul looked around and felt very lonely. It was

something he hadn't felt in decades—had thought he'd escaped, and yet here it was, filling his heart like smoke.

They walked home slowly. There were candles placed in front of a tree at one house, with stuffed bears. They stopped, gazing at the display

"I want to give them my sympathy," Paul said and turned towards it.

"I'm sorry," Paul said when a man answered the door. "I'm sorry for your loss."

"Did you know Sherry?" the man said. "I'm the one who said she could go. I should have told her to come straight home. But how could I know?"

A few blocks later, Ann Mary looked down to the right and saw a bunch of cars parked in the street, and people gathered. They turned that way. A woman carrying a casserole fell into step beside them. "Did you know Clare?"

"No," said Ann Mary. "But we feel so saddened by all this." She hesitated. "It could have happened to anyone."

"It could have been all of us," the neighbour agreed. "So strange. She was just filling in for the regular bus driver. That's the kind of thing that will drive Bill crazy, won't it? The hand of fate, the hand of God, dumb luck, whatever. What if she'd run late. Or run early. Hard to think about."

"Very hard," Paul agreed. The woman left, and they continued walking. Finally Paul said, "If it had been *our* bus with *our* people, there would have been no doubt." He didn't finish the thought.

"Paul, this wasn't it," Ann Mary sighed.

"The church is dividing up," he answered. "Those who believe it happened without us, and those who believe we got our math wrong. Who's right? The ones who can't do math or the ones who think God skipped over us?"

She signed. "Jonah is upset because he lost his friend. Why are you upset?"

Paul was silent for a moment. "Don't you wonder? That we might have been wrong?"

"It would be unbearable," she said slowly. "To think what you're thinking. Pray, Paul. This is not the time to stop talking to God."

Jonah let them come in. "But be careful about the dogs," he warned.

"We have to discuss the dogs," Ann Mary said firmly. "The big ones have to stay outside. At least for a while."

"No," Jonah said.

He seemed, suddenly, older. Ann Mary studied him. "At least the ones that are bigger than Gina," she said finally.

He nodded, and the crowd of dogs followed him to the back door. He grabbed the bigger ones and pushed them through to the outside, where they began to race around.

"Jonah," Ann Mary said. "What can we do? I've lost something too, but we have to hold on to each other. I know that. What can I do to hold on to you?"

Jonah felt a small release in his heart, and he hated it. "I want to see where Joey died," he answered.

His mother rocked back, noting that he had said "died," not "ascended."

"Yes,'" she said.

They were quiet on the drive out of town. They took the road that led uphill, along the back valley roads. They came to a curve that showed them a smashed spot ahead:

flown trees, tires, scraps of metal. There was a wooden barricade with a blinking light closing off one lane. Jonah reminded himself that it had happened a day ago. That seemed too much time; he didn't want to get so far away from when Joey was alive.

They pulled up to the wooden barricade, a puny thing; what was the point? Part of the guardrail was out, of course; but the wooden sawhorse would keep nothing from going over.

They got out of the car and stood looking at the path of the tornado—bent trees, snapped trees, and a stripped path—clear but brown and aching—straight through.

The weather was changing again; they could feel the wind scraping against their eyes.

Gina had taken Buster with her, Joey's dog, to see Joey's last place alive. Jonah noticed the dog dangling from Gina's embrace, one leg thrown out straight, not able to fit in the crook of her arm.

"He was right here when it happened," Jonah said. "Probably looking out the window the wrong way. I mean, on the other side of the bus, where nothing was happening."

"It's getting dark," Ann Mary said. "We should go."

"Just clouds," Paul said. "You know how the weather's been lately. We could use the rain."

"Mom?" Gina said, pointing at where the valley was narrow. The trees were rippling.

They all looked and paused. Ann Mary put her hand on Gina's shoulder, gripping too hard, but Gina leaned into her, gripping Buster too hard.

"Good Lord," Paul whispered. His voice rose on the last word. Ann Mary squinted, leaned into the wind, and looked at her husband's beatific face. Her heart rose, too.

Jonah thought only of Joey, caught in the grip of the wind, and how much he had missed him already, and how impossible it would be to go on missing him.

The wooden saw horse flew away—out ahead of them, like something jerked by a magnet. It looked like a wide, dirty cloud dipping its head at them . . . a whirlwind, a spout. It was rushing towards them and as it rushed it got broader and thicker and there was a sound—a big shout in the background of the other shouts.

As Jonah watched he saw two thin spouts split off from the massive centre, one to each side. They tipped away from each other and then magnetically the feet of their spouts drew back in to the centre and the high wide whirling wash of it took a breath and rushed forward.

The horizon twitched and rolled towards them and the renewed tornado bore down on them, shrieking.

It took up leftover trees and pieces of earth; things were lifted and swirled, intact, for half a rotation and then they went to pieces, the smallest parts swinging up ahead of the largest. A mailbox from down the road faced forward, standing upright, as if it were being shooed.

The lifting up was stunning and fast. The tornado jiggled to the right and swept up trees and a rock and a baler. Joey thought he saw birds being pulled in, because he saw things pulled in now, not just lifted up. An old boundary wall got pulled up like a carpet, and a small wood outbuilding fell apart and got swept up all at the same time, rising in pieces almost neatly disassembled. And was there a man in there too? He was sure now he could see people rotating up the wide whirl of it, some upside down, some with their arms out, as if to steady themselves. There was a dog, too, and it seemed that its mouth was moving, that it was barking, all astonished, as it was turned and disappeared. The dog hurt his heart.

His mother started forward, then looked back at them, laughed, said something that couldn't be heard, then faced back into it. Her hair was straight up now, blown up.

He could barely breathe. With all that wind, there seemed to be too little air. He was afraid but he was thrilled, too. His father, bent over, tried to make his way to Ann Mary, and Gina fell over and then fell up, and the dog ran to the side and then got knocked over. His mother turned again and her face was splendid.

His father reached an arm out to him and grinned. He was rising, that's all he knew, and his heart, already beating wildly, beat hopefully. He reached his hand out and grabbed, feeling his father's hands close on his. He shouted for joy. His back arced as he rose. He held his eyes open. It was glory, it was glory, it was glory.

THE ESCAPE ARTIST

I am dizzy with height, breathless. The wind up here is so strong it has fingers, fists, walls, even waterfalls in it.

The rope—thick as my wrist—is curved like an inverted horizon. Einstein rules here; for left to right, top to bottom, no plane is straight. The wind takes part of the rope and pushes it, slow motion, as if to shake me off. But I can resist the wind.

It's so high up here, with the rope stretched between the Twin Towers, that I know the truth: distance is the secret at the heart of things.

I am afraid of heights; I am in love with heights. Only someone this terrified would climb so high, so far, so free, so pure.

I never look down. Looking down has the fatal flaw of attraction in it. I like the moment when the rope is set, when it slides in the wind, and I pause on the edge of the roof. The sound of the air blows every other thought away and all I see around me is space without confines, just space—and the rope—and there, appearing just in the centre—Gabriel.

Damn smack on the rope, riding it, his hand

outstretched as ever, expecting me. The wind at a pitch, the rope swaying, and Gabriel, his wings folded flat against his back tight as a fingernail, or outspread partly, never as large as you'd think and light and densely etched, each feather sometimes moving like a living thing as he unfolds, unfolds.

I walked the first rope because I needed to overcome fear, because the things you fear control you, and the second rope—ten stories higher—to prove my resolve. Every rope has been higher, longer, more inhabited by height and I won't lie, I can no longer tell the difference between love and fear.

I know I'm always afraid that this will be the last rope my nerves can handle, or that I'm now more enslaved by the need to triumph over fear than I was by fear itself. It's possible, always possible.

I suspect my fear is no longer pure.

The third walk—at a height of roughly 500 feet—was the first time I saw a figure on my rope, turned and waiting for me.

I stood on the windowsill, my fingers backed against a pane of glass, trying to place him, who he was and why he was there. I already knew enough to look only out—out, never down—so my eyes were trapped by him and I thought at first it would be impossible to step out, that two people on the rope would be a disaster, that I would force him down or it would be—at the least—a breach of etiquette I knew nothing about, because every rope I had stepped on I stepped on alone.

It was the flutter at his back that decided me, the sly protrusion of his flexing wing. My foot stepped out, the arch of it fisted on the rope, holding it like a hand grasp, so that when the rope swayed I held on to it with my foot. The trick is not to fight it; the trick is to believe that air is the floor of your life.

Gabriel was naked. How was it ever possible to pretend angels would be clothed? Are birds? How would a hummingbird fly in a gauzy white gown?

The naked, winged man on the rope had a casual air. He stood at ease, with grace and friendliness, with interest. I moved slowly on the rope.

There was a slight wind and I was still relatively new to ropes then. I was grateful in a way to keep my eyes on him. When I first stepped out I saw the buildings behind him, framing him, but as I reached him the space around him freed up, so there was air. All ropes seem curved that way, their centres independent of their moorings, as if the bridge a rope makes is itself the impossible country, Oz in the sky.

Gabriel, that first time, let me approach without saying a word. Surprises are so much more impressive in silence. He had dark, straight heavy hair parted in the center, falling down to the point where his jawbone turned up to his ear. His eyes were brown and direct, not quite almond-shaped, and his nose was almost Indian, strong and sharp. There was no crease anywhere on his face, nor on his body, which was muscular, narrow at the hips and dark in the loins. His feet were beautifully formed, resting almost without impression on the rope.

The wing that had flexed when I first saw him opened and I caught a faint ripple of muscles on his shoulder as it did. The wing opened straight out, the way a sparrow's did, without the bend that artists like to put in it. It was paler than his skin when open—a beige colour faintly streaked with cream. The feathers were small and it was possible when looking at the wing as a whole to think it resembled a shell, changing at the edges into transparency. I was soon close enough to see the way each feather topped the one in front of it and how the skin thickened where the wing sloped into his shoulder. There it was the consistency of muscle with a thin opaque covering. When I looked at the feathers I wanted to stroke them lightly; when I looked at the wing I wanted to fly.

Tremors fluttered the wing in waves, as if he were idly clenching and unclenching muscles, and it appeared to me that each feather was separately operated and intricately managed.

He smiled as I looked at him, waiting for my study of his wings to end. Then he held his hand out to me, also beautifully extended, a hand without callus or scar, its fingers shaped to a roundness at the tip. I refused his hand; I had no doubt that his touch would be unnerving.

"Will you take one step with me?" he asked, and his voice had a rich, surprising depth to it. It was a sliding voice, it slipped into your head and loosened speculations.

The sky behind him now was a flat aluminum. It seemed so flat and I seemed so high and yet the effect of it—I could feel my heart beat through the soles of my feet, linked with the strands of the rope—the effect was to make me feel like the centre of the universe.

Of course, that's why I love the rope: Time is concentrated. Your life is stark, reduced to each minute, each move; every second matters as it never matters on the ground. You are aware of your pulse, the sweat on your skin. Things that have no consequence on earth matter with a vengeance in the sky. You cannot live by default, only by choice.

So when I heard him speak in that sliding voice, I stepped backwards on my rope and said No.

He turned his head half away from me, seeking out the flat gray sky. The wind hooked high around him, he leaned into it, and his wings opened and fluttered so fast they blurred before fitting neatly back together. "Do you think you could dance," he asked, "this high up?"

I felt the rope under my foot begin to wriggle, shifting in the wind in unpredictable impulses. "Hold my hand," he said. "I can help you."

For one brief moment his voice gave me hints of a promise, release from the rope. But even then I noted how my foot relaxed—and how I was starting to lean clumsily forward into the curve of the rope where Gabriel stood. I had lost concentration. He was not offering me grace.

"Are you a fallen angel?" I asked.

He smiled. "Half-fallen," he said.

That was all we said, that first time, because I backed up along the rope, till I stood firm against the window. He had smiled for a while, watching me, and then stopped smiling. His head turned into the breeze and the sky. He had a quality of waiting that was impressive; I have never waited well.

I was curious whether he would be there the next time, and as I prepared the rope a few weeks later, the thought of him standing in the sky—a sky closer by another ten stories—was always in my mind.

I am very careful about choosing the rope days. No rain, small winds, no sun. The light has to spread out in space without disruption: that means cloudy skies.

A dusty sky this time, brushed here and there with washed-out slate as ranges of clouds lined the distance, mountains to be climbed someday, shifting Everests.

My hair was slicked right to my head, my body taut in tights, my arms outspread for steadiness, and I stepped out again.

Gabriel was there, small as a statue as I took my first step. Still as a statue, a weightless one, barely bending the rope. As I walked towards him, I could feel the line's resistance alter.

I stopped a yard away from him. "Gabriel," I called.

"That's not my name." He crossed his arms on his chest. "Gabriel's a name in one of your stories," he said. "Not mine."

"Gabriel. Why are you waiting for me?"

"I've been watching you. You draw me to you. Your eyes are the colour of the sky today. Please give me your hand."

"Why? Will you show me the sky?" I asked.

His head dipped sideways. "I can show you the world."

He glanced down and for a split-second my eyes followed his. My right arm dipped, my balance faltered, I was stricken with a hollow feeling. I threw my eyes up again, past him, to hang my sight on a cloud; that cloud and I became the centre; the rest of the world moved and we stayed steady. My arm regained its balance.

"I wouldn't hurt you." His voice tempted me, and I believed him. For that my arms relaxed and I bent to the earth. With an effort I stopped that; I ceased to believe.

"What do you want from me?"

"Please. Take my hand."

"I'd lose my balance. I'm sure of it."

"It's not a question of balance, not really. See? I can look anywhere." And to prove it, he looked down.

"Please stop looking down. You could cause me to hurt myself."

He looked back up at me. He had a simple, clear gaze. I admired his features, the purity, the classicism of them. Perhaps such things belonged to his kind, above gravity of all sorts. I had to balance myself, right foot back, shift weight, right foot forward.

"All falling things fall to earth," he said sweetly, once again gazing down.

I was learning to control the impulse to follow his eyes. I locked myself to the horizon and said, "How marvellous it must be, to step out in the sky." The clouds were rushing towards me; it was windier than I liked.

"It's everything you could imagine," he whispered.

On that we both paused, our eyes ranged in different directions. He blinked and then opened his eyes. "I don't have terror of any kind," he said gently. "Just a thought, that goes on forever. A single train of thought. What would I be?" He gestured slightly downwards. "That's all. I don't know why it occurs to me, but it does. If there were only the sky, I would be content, I suppose. But if I look down, at them . . . at you, I start to wonder, *What would I be?*"

I knew I had to get off the rope. His voice was so soothing, so musically sad, I began to feel the sadness myself, a longing for Earth.

"We could help each other," he said as I backed away. "We want the same thing."

My heart was bumping into itself; the rapid beats

threatened to make me dizzy. He didn't lean towards me or follow me as I left, but kept his steady stare on my face, as if he were still talking.

When I thought, later, of going up again, and having him there again, and feeling again that longing to rush through the air without check, I grew frightened. He made death feel fond. I had always respected my own willingness to be afraid—*that* had given me courage, not the fight to overcome it.

But it is a fight somehow. I know very well that the Twin Towers is as high as I can go, and that he will be there. In the back of my mind is a decision I can't make, a question I can't even ask. I would have gone up again anyway, I'm sure of it, but I know that this time I've come to see Gabriel.

The wind smells of iron and glass. This high up there is a different climate from below. It's private that way.

If he wasn't here I could walk from one end to the other, I could bend in the wind and defy the cold that's different—stripped—from the weather below.

But he is here and I move to him, my arms outspread, walking to him, to hear his voice. I have to continue, despite Gabriel—or despite my feeling that Gabriel has twisted the conditions of my test. He has introduced melancholy; I've caught it from him, that yearning to reach not the cause of fear, but the end of fear.

Once again, he smiles at me from the curve of the rope. Again, I stop a yard away. He sighs. "Watching you is lovely," he says. "You're so careful, so concentrated. I envy that."

"Why?"

"This is as far as I've been able to get," he says, his eyes bright and warm. "I can't go any farther."

"I don't understand."

He holds his hand out, friendliness reaching for me like tentacles. "I need a body to weigh me down."

The wind has a sound to it, a long sigh. It makes my neck prickle.

"You want to fall," he says. "That's why you're here."

"No."

"You're in love with falling, you dream about it, it's in your head like a song."

"No."

"All the time below is meaningless; this is all that matters. How sweet, how clear, how consequential. We are a pair," he croons, lifting his wing out along with his hand. "You come up and look there, and there, and there." He sweeps the sky with his wing. "But this isn't what matters to you, is it?"

My knees tremble, I can feel a thrill translating to them from the rope. I have always believed that I was superior to fear because I swallowed it whole each time I set foot on my rope. But—it was true, it wasn't the sky or the wind or the clouds that drew me up; it was the bursting out, through, down, the long straight moment that stretched between me and the land. I always went higher to stretch the moment longer. The thought of it makes my mouth dry, my eyes water, it gazes at me, it's almost carnal in its itch.

The sigh the wind makes is resolute, it gathers in a pitch like a voice around my tongue.

Gabriel, clothed in serenity, holds himself gently on the rope. He moves toward me. He's close enough now that my hand and his hand would meet if extended.

THE INNER CITY

The rope keeps moving, shaking itself solemnly, and my feet dance with it. The curve of the rope is heavier than it has been; it compels me to Gabriel, like a bright light in a long tunnel.

Gabriel holds his hand out, palm up, a plea for my company, my consent. I want to touch it, to see what density there is in it—light, cold, silky, firm? A cloud pours itself into a dark flower and flows into a wing.

"No," I say, "no," and I walk back on the rope to the roof of my world, and I cut the rope so that it falls like a bridge collapsing, and Gabriel opens his wings as if he doesn't even need them and he stays there, poised where the rope should be, as if I would return, as if a time must come when I'll return.

THE LARGE PEOPLE

Patricia Sweetman saw a bowler hat on the ground, its rim just barely out of the ground, and she went to it, bent over and studied it. There was dirt in the crease on top, more dirt on the sides, but for all that it looked fresh and unharmed. She reached out and lightly brushed off the dirt, making it neat again, and considered taking it home, to give to someone or perhaps even wear it herself in a style inappropriate for her age.

She lifted it up and saw, underneath, on the ground, like a small hill rising, a man's head of hair, parted on the side. The part was clean and white, the hair was dark brown. She froze. At first she thought she was mistaken, that she was suggestible, that no one's head would be stuck in the ground, but then she thought, "Why not?" In this incredible world, why not? With all the weirdoes running around, uncaught and even undisclosed, why not someone who buried a man standing up, though— as she straightened up and looked around, noting the condition of the soil, the sprouting plants, the rooted bushes—though nothing looked at all disturbed. It all felt quite natural.

Of course she couldn't get it out of her mind, so every day she returned, just to see, and every day the head of the man rose a little higher as if he were indeed another plant anxious to get going now that the earth was warm.

And then she noticed another hat, a cap really, come pushing up out of the soil, and then a beehive hairdo, a baldish head, a scarf tied around the slicked back hair on another head, until in all there were almost two dozen of them, now with their eyes above ground, looking serious and patient, until their chins tucked free and they moved their heads slightly, observing the world with faintly impatient airs.

Sometimes the head with the bowler nodded slightly when she showed up. One of the women winked at her once. Soon their shoulders were above ground and she saw they were all dressed in business attire—even the women wore suit jackets, clean shirts; the men wore ties, except for the one in casual business wear, who wore a sports jacket and polo shirt, but very crisp and pricey looking. By the time their waists were showing she herself wore her best clothes, or really, to be honest, her better clothes because she was retired and her best clothes were out of date. But she was determined to honour them by dressing as they did. And it was interesting, too, how wearing business clothes again made her feel a bit more efficient. Uselessly efficient.

By then, one man and two women had asked her how the land was doing around there, subject to breakage and contaminations, and Patricia wasn't sure about the way the questions were asked so she said, "Pretty much the same as yesterday," and they would put down their newspapers (they all had newspapers) and then look into the distance. She followed their eyes and saw a haze just down the road, where the city sat like a blister. Her heart gave a little lurch; she had worked there and missed the sense of importance and irritation the city gave her; if they went there, she would go with them. Why not? Whatever these people were, they weren't ordinary and she herself had been reading more and more about the organic lifestyle anyhow, so she had the feeling they were topical. For a woman who had once been lower management, being topical felt almost lusty. And the fact that it was all so unusual made her happy. She felt less inconsequential; she felt part of the new order, and she imagined the new order would be fundamentally daring. She could be daring.

When the last one of them shook his feet free from the earth, she had her own briefcase and wore a suitable jacket and skirt. All of them were carrying briefcases and cellular phones and paper cups of coffee that had grown beside them in the last few days, steaming in the morning, the vapour rising from the neatly folded dib in the plastic cup.

They assembled gently on the road. Remarkably, the dirt didn't cling to them; perhaps it was the peculiar texture of their business wear, which seemed wrinkle-resistant and smooth without being shiny. Their shoes were polished. Their white shirts were spotless. The women—there were six women in addition to over a dozen men—wore skirt suits and low-heeled shoes.

Patricia would have bet that the women carried chai lattes, and that the men were evenly split between coffee black and cappuccino with a double espresso shot. That had been the rule where she worked. But she'd retired five years ago; perhaps the caffeine fashions had changed.

Her own hand was empty. She felt faintly embarrassed and bent down to pluck a daisy from the side of the road. When she straightened up she saw that they were looking at her. She bent down slowly and put the daisy back on the ground.

The last of the large people—for they were well over seven feet in height and were proportionately thicker than normal people, too, giving them a substantial impression, a width that was almost tree-like—the last of them had reached the road. The man with the bowler asked, "Are we all here then?" and someone answered, "Yes, Roland, we're all here."

They strode off, in twos and threes, casually rippling together as if they had no weight, and they quickly passed fields, then houses, then strip malls. The city rose ahead of them like rows of mountains, its spires the peaks, the streets the valleys, and around them, shouldering their stride into the city, through the industrial suburbs, were the high-flowering ranks of electrical towers, the granite squat of generators and transformers. Tufts of drying grasses sat disconsolately on broken macadam, with exhausted branches flung nearby. The sky was a pale blue almost white.

Patricia had to jog to keep up with them, their strides were so much longer. The road turned into a street and then an avenue. They walked sturdily and quickly up to the first glass and marble tower, its windows shaded gray like a building hidden behind sunglasses, and here the group divided, half moving forward along the avenue while the rest (including Patricia) went into the building. These marched without comment past the security guards and the main desk, up to the elevators, where they broke apart without a word, standing in front of different elevators—unwilling, she thought, to tax the weight limits. She had followed the bowler hat, who seemed to be in charge. When the doors opened, the elevator's passengers took one startled glance and scurried out, peering at the massive forms from lowered heads.

The large people stepped into the elevator, allowing room for Patricia, and pressed the button for the 30th floor. She noticed that the man in the bowler hat was looking at her with raised eyebrows. "I'm Roland," he said.

"Patricia," she said.

"Ciceline," the woman who stood next to him said. "Thank you for joining us."

"Are we going to a meeting?" Patricia said hopefully; she missed the self-importance of meetings.

"We are going to take over," Roland said evenly. "Things have come to a pass."

The phrase itself said nothing, and rather than display what might be perceived as ignorance, she merely nodded. Taking over would change what had come to a pass and it would all become clearer. She had no objection to it; she was old enough to have seen what had been and what was; and she disliked, sometimes, the world as it was.

The doors pinged open—and all the other doors on the other elevators pinged open simultaneously—and a beautiful kind of orchestrated step forward happened as the large people put their right feet out at once and kept walking, striding, wonderfully moving together into the corridor. Patricia was proud to be part of this movement;

and she felt a little smug, too, as if she'd been selected.

They swept past the receptionist and into a meeting room where a dozen men sat around a table with coffee and a tray of bagels in front of them. There was a Power Point presentation going on; the screen read: Projected Highway Miles. The lines on the chart went upwards, in thousands of miles, a figure that astonished Patricia. Thousands of miles per year?

The large people stepped through doorways the way anyone else would step through a hatchway: right foot, right arm, body. They bent down a little, to avoid hitting their heads.

One by one they assembled behind the men in their chairs, who turned, surprised at what was going on. The man at the Power Point looked around the room, trying to figure out whether this disruption was something he was supposed to handle. The men at the table were shifting, looking around, whispering to each other, but uneasily noncommittal. The man at the head of the table rose up and said, "I don't know who you people are." Everyone looked at him expectantly.

Roland nodded at another of the large men. "That's the one," he said. "Take him out, Anselm." The large man with the brown hair and the brown suit stepped neatly forward, placed his enormous hand on the shoulder of what Patricia presumed was the president of the company, and took him outside, protesting intensely, his head bent back to look up into Anselm's impassive face.

The room rustled with indecision. Roland turned off the projector and addressed them: "No more invasions," he said. "For every mile you pave, a mile of land must be restored."

"We have a *contract*," one man said testily. "Restoring land is someone else's job." Immediately, two of the large men moved towards him and placed their fingers on his shoulders.

The man narrowed his eyes. "Get your hands off me," he said. "I'm calling security." He reached for his cell phone.

"Take him away," Roland said. Two of the large men grabbed him and they disappeared to the hallway. "Take them all away," Roland added, and the businessmen jumped up, some arguing but many feeling that it was better to give in than to protest. Patricia felt a small qualm. She had assumed the large people were benign: were they? She sat down quickly in a vacated seat, her hands in her lap.

"We'll have lunch now," Roland said, clearing the table of notepads and notebooks, of handouts and charts. The door opened and some of his cohorts entered with trays piled high with money of all denominations, as well as mayonnaise and salad dressings. Roland sat down with apparent pleasure, took a plate and fork and began to select bills and pile them on. "Help yourselves," he said, and the other large people came in and sat down, leaning over for plates and food. "I prefer the twenties," he said, glancing at Patricia. "Not as crisp as the fifties, not so soft as the singles." His plate was now quite hefty with bills, and he poured Italian dressing on them, careful not to dribble over the sides. He sat back and began to eat, chewing vigorously and thoughtfully. "Eat up," he said, motioning with his fork.

Patricia reached out and took some of the hundreds—she would have to take something to be polite and these seemed cleaner. She chose blue cheese dressing and decided to roll up a bill with a wad of dressing in it and eat it like an hors d'oeuvre. It wasn't bad; the dressing made it all that much easier. Eating money! she thought. Eating money! She was inordinately pleased.

Roland and the large people ate quickly and quietly, their heads lowered, concentrating on the task at hand. When he was done, Roland put down his flatware, cleaned off his hands, and rose.

"What about the rest of it?" Patricia asked, looking at the leftover money.

"It will grow," Roland said without interest. Ciceline came into the room, glanced around, and placed a small green ball on the platter of money, put her newspaper over it, then emptied a glass of water over the whole thing. Patricia followed them as they left. She glanced back; the stain from the green ball was spreading through the newspaper already. The fibers in the newspaper were starting to move.

"Roland," Patricia said. "I know I should have asked earlier, but I need to be clear. Are you going to harm anyone?"

He stopped to look at her without emotion. "Yes," he said. "This is a war."

She bowed her head. "Am I on the right side?" she asked quietly. She had always believed in being forthright and honest whenever possible.

"How can there be a right side in war?" he asked reasonably. "It's just that each side wants to live."

She wanted to live, too, brazenly. For a moment she doubted that she was doing the right thing, but her feet continued after Roland. She had watched the large people grow, so she was naturally attached to them. And she had always had a complex reaction to working in the city: some days she loathed it, some days it felt more real than her own life. It seemed to her that she had been, most of the time, on the road between the self she was in the city and the self she was outside it, between structure and order. She had stopped moving back and forth when she retired, but from that point on she had felt dull and compromised, arrested. With Roland she felt strong and certain and ahead of everyone else. It was, no doubt, not the thing to base a decision on, but she hadn't felt this empowered in years. She would go with Roland.

They met up with the others back on the street. The large people stood idly, not in rows, looking at a spot along the avenue. There, right on the corner, a small dry cleaner's shop was absurdly lopsided, its back wall up in the air, its front wall tipping toward the street as a small crowd watched, quietly waiting behind yellow caution strips placed by the emergency squads.

The building gave a small but obvious lurch.

"That's good," Anselm said. "Almost there." They began to walk slowly towards the store, and people moved out of their way if they saw them, with a look of surprise on their faces.

A cop watched them carefully, then came over and spoke to Roland. "Heard a report," he said. "Of some big people—pardon me, not a judgement—disrupting a meeting." He looked at Roland. "That's what dispatch said. Disrupting a meeting. Would that be you?"

Roland nodded. "Shareholders," he said. "Stock disagreement."

"Thought so," the officer said. "As far as I know, those

stocks are outside the law anyway. Just checking." He nodded and moved towards the shifting building, calling out, "Just get back now, behind the line. Never saw a building collapse before? What are you, from out of town?"

The dry cleaner's, Patricia could now see, rested on a pale green slab of some kind. She craned her neck forward and Anselm, noticing her difficulty, pushed aside everyone in front of her so she could see it unobstructed. It was the colour of new spring growth, and it perfectly filled the lot the dry cleaner's store stood on. There was a sound of breaking glass and a groan from the roof of the cleaner's, echoed by a groan of excitement from the bystanders. "Move back! Move back!" the police cried, and it was just in time, for the building suddenly heaved up a few more inches and toppled bulkily into the street.

The green shelf below it had sprouted up a foot or so. Anselm had a smile on his face. "Is that a plant?" Patricia asked. She had an urge to touch it but the police blocked the way.

Anselm's smile increased. "An office plant," he said. "Evergreen."

She liked the mass and decisiveness of the large people, as anyone would who had always been seen as irrelevant; she liked how they brought with them a sense of turnover and vitality and a lack of cant. They would not pretend they were good for the economy or good for the average man or woman, she thought; they would not have secret accounts or back room deals or documents that covered their lies with tired, boring, overworked words. There was a little bit of outlaw about them, and a little bit of saviour. She had to talk to herself for a moment to admit that it was the outlaw part that appealed the most, and she was too old for outlawry—or so she had thought.

Roland moved off and some of the large people went with him, moving down side streets to the back of some commercial buildings. They walked slowly, looking at surfaces and signs. Ciceline bent down to look at a browned bush and some browned weeds; she turned, walked back a few yards, and knocked over a fire hydrant to water them.

Farther on they caught up to some of the ones who had broken off from the group earlier. The man in casual dress—the one who wore a sports jacket rather than a suit—faced the side of a grooved, white stone building, his body right smack up against the ridges, so tight that Patricia thought it must be painful. His arms were splayed out, his fingers in the channels around each stone. Those fingers, she saw, were very long, stretching along the ridges—even as she watched they stretched further, inching along and, she thought, catching in the small textures of the material. Yes, adhering. His fingers were turning into vines. His body pressed and flattened into the building, his face tightened into a pale sunflower, his suit changed into leaves, his trunk into a stalk, even as she watched, so that she had to squint to see what was left of him, still hidden behind the growth. A shoot rose from the top of his head, sliding up to the second-floor windows.

Anselm saw her gaze. "He'll make his way in, under the concrete, into the beams, around the windows and into the walls. As they walk around, sure that the floors are solid, he'll be licking at the materials, putting out a leaf or a pointed tendril."

She raised her eyebrows. "Water and sun?" she asked.

"He'll find water easily; there are pipes and sinks. And the windows—windows will find the sun for him."

Her mind became filled with the image of the plant spreading and pushing its way through the walls, the floors, its relentless small separations loosening a bolt, a beam. "It will bring the building down," she said.

"Everything comes down eventually," he replied.

"No one will know about it. In time."

"That's the problem with time. There's never enough time in the present to know the present. We keep growing."

"Someone could get hurt."

"Someone always gets hurt. It's the fault of time, which always pushes to the end. Doesn't it? Always to the end."

She winced, suddenly aware of her own push to the end. She tucked in the edges of her own thinking, to compensate. Nature always took the long view, and the long view had no sorrow. Personally, she didn't like sorrow either.

They were heading out of town again, back, she supposed, to the area where they had originally grown. Was it over? she wondered with faint despair. She had hoped for so much more.

They passed a gas station, where two of the large people stepped away from the group. Patricia saw a large woman plant a bamboo-like stalk next to a drainpipe; she saw a large man leave his newspaper against a pump. But there was no confrontation; and she was disappointed. Were the thrills of the day already done?

The remaining large people moved off a side road that Patricia knew led towards the town dump. When they reached it, they all spread out and she lost sight of Roland. She saw Anselm skirt around the edge of the pit and followed him into the hardscrabble brush around it. She found him bent over a black bag of garbage, pushing it gently, scraping away at the packed soil around it.

"Anselm?" she asked gently, and he looked at her and nodded. She came up and leaned over the garbage, but as she studied it, she saw that it had a root. She said, "It's a plant?" and he answered, "It's a new kind of plant." She pushed at it and it yielded slightly, as a heavy bag of garbage would do. "But why?" she asked finally.

"They won't notice it," he said.

Anselm tapped the plant gently, even (Patricia thought) affectionately. "Have you planted a lot?" she asked. She looked at him, cocking her head. Had he worn a hat? Had his hair been longer? What had happened to the coffee cup and newspapers he'd held? She looked away, viewing the landfill, looking not into the pit but along the sides, where here and there the large people moved and stopped, sowing seeds, leaving roots. She liked the idea of the rest of them leaving traces of full-force green in among the rust and oilcans, among the cardboard boxes and plastic bottles.

Anselm was looking at her. "Our time is almost over."

"You mean for today?" she asked fearfully. The idea that tomorrow would come and go without them was ferociously sad.

"Yes, today is over for us," he said, and she appreciated the delicacy of his answer. It didn't sound like he regretted it; it sounded like the day was enough for him, a concept that made Patricia shiver. The large people met up again, and she noted that they looked a little frayed, and that various items of theirs were gone. The hats, for instance, and the newspapers and coffee cups, and a handkerchief poking out of a pocket.

The sun hung low in the sky as they gathered on a spot beyond the garbage dump, listening to the keening of the seagulls swirling in the air. Roland was missing; it was Anselm and Ciceline and a few others. They moved languidly away from the dump to a small stand of trees. There they stood until one by one they sat down or leaned against a tree trunk. Patricia sat with them as the sunset bleached the sky. They were no longer large; they had lost bulk and seemed to shrivel in front of her. She saw their bodies relax and their hands grow still. Once they were completely settled, their arms and features arranged, and their eyes shut, Patricia watched over them until the sunset and the moon began to rise. By then, their figures were dim and slumped, and she decided she didn't want to watch them as they slid back into the earth. But she did want something of theirs to take forward, so she bent and plucked off the buttons on their shirts and jackets. By midnight they were thin as leaves upon the ground, and she left.

The next day she went back to where she had first found them and planted buttons in the ground, got mulch and spread it around, and began to grow herbs around and between them, hoping that soon there would be another crop. People passing by noted her efforts, and the small shapes of flowers and herbs on the set of the hill, and thought nothing of it, for old women like to tend their gardens; what else is there for them to do as time advances and nature takes its course?

AFTER IMAGES

A survey I conducted on Water Street concludes that 58 percent of Americans think it is probably 58 degrees out, while 22 think it is probably 54, and the remainder aren't sure.

For the first time in weather history this month, the percentage of people thinking it is 58 degrees is exactly 58. This happens, we are told, on average of once every six months. You won't see that happening again until probably late fall or early winter, although polls also show that a majority of people think there won't be any winter next year at all.

That was the gist of my segment on last night's news. Today I got called into the office. "We're getting complaints," the news manager said. He's a fat man and one ear is lower than the other, giving him a quizzical look. "People say your segments are insulting."

"How many people said that? Maybe they're just the kind of people who complain. You have to ask the people who *don't* complain what they think."

"No, I don't," the manager said. "I don't have to do anything."

"Poor choice of words," I conceded. "I merely meant: balance. We strive for balance."

"No, we don't," the manager said.

"What do you want, sir?" I asked humbly.

"Relevance. Nobody wants a poll on what the temperature might be. They want to know what the temperature *is*, and move on to sports."

I bowed my head.

And by the way, how accurate are the polls? We asked 40 people and 20 said not accurate and 20 said accurate. Which means, according to our off-screen analyst, that any survey, tally, census, or sampling of the public would itself be only half-accurate, since the public is divided in the concept of accuracy itself and is therefore unreliable.

But is this really so? We asked a former employee of Burton & Pudge Poll Company, which compiles statistics on the surveys themselves, how surveys are measured. This employee, who prefers to remain anonymous, says that polls in general get three different results if the interviewee is asked the same question in three different ways. In response, Burton & Pudge representatives stated that this in itself points out the refinements of the polling process itself, which recognizes that only 30 percent of respondents hear all the words in a sentence, a figure that has been verified by having test subjects write down all the words in a sentence in reverse order so as to eliminate rote repetition. Ten percent do not write down the word "not" in a sentence that contains it.

On the other hand, 13 percent put it in when it wasn't there to begin with.

This is how the polling industry comes up with the plus-

or-minus 3 percent variance, since misunderstandings on either side of the scale are 3 percent away from cancelling themselves out.

I was invited to the office again. The manager said, "That was not what we had in mind. Polls should be fun. If they can't be fun, what's the point of it?"

I considered that, and thought that was a very good observation.

According to research by Wallup and Pye Interview Associates, facial expression is more accurate than verbal expression, at least when the face itself is aware it is lying. Most times it is not lying and then all we want to know is: does a flat face like what we're saying or not? That's simple enough.

Sticking one's tongue out is a no; smiling is a yes, unless the eyes are squinting, in which case it's no again. A shake of the head, no; a nod, yes. But beyond that— what is the nose saying? (Flaring, sniffing, snorting?) We have also calibrated the ears, since some people, sociopaths especially, confine their telling expressions to the earlobe. They may pass all the tests checking the muscles of the lips, the eyebrows, the eyelids, the nostril, but the ear tightens and the lobe clenches. That is a lie.

"The ear?" the co-anchor said, suspiciously.

We can also track your voice, you know; we can tell the truth of what you're saying.

"The ear?" he repeated. "I don't believe the ear even has muscles."

"I don't care about that, really. Maybe it's the cartilage that quivers."

Ha.

He waved me off, also a telling gesture, but a little blunt. It takes no special education to understand that.

I turned to address him, sharing my airtime. "Did you know the way you dress also reveals a lot? And I don't mean, do you have style, do you have money. I mean, this is a person who has no imagination, this is a person who fantasizes. Okay, you say, that's easy. But I must add, when you lie, your clothes don't fit as well. Unless you stay absolutely still, and that's a dead giveaway. A person who doesn't shift around during interrogation is a person hiding something."

"Interrogation?"

"Well yes, what did you think I was talking about?"

His eyes narrowed. He slowly put his hand in his pocket. As if he had something, yes. He thought he had an instrument that could deflect me. His nostrils flared.

His ear twitched.

I was getting the hang of being called into the office. I hung my head immediately and said, "Boss, what should I do?"

"You have to know what the public wants," he said. "You have to have the knack for it. What is it that gets our goat? Scandal, crime, the all-chocolate diet. Death and taxes, they get everyone interested. Do something on taxes."

I'm not interested in taxes.

The final test of any poll of course is what the dead say about dying. That's the poll we want and never get. The dead, as far as polls are concerned, have nothing to say about death once the body freezes up, but right after death, especially that moment we like to call "instantaneous death," we find it is still possible to get a few questions in.

Shortly after a local criminal was guillotined, his head in a basket, a sharply observant reporter noticed that the eyes of the head were slowly closing. He rushed to the head with a microphone.

"Excuse me, Sir, how do you feel?" the reporter asked.

The eyes flickered open and stared at the reporter. There was a slight movement of the tongue.

The reporter was excited. "If you feel pain, Sir, blink your eyes! Blink on a scale of one to ten to tell us how much pain." He stuck his microphone at the head's lips. Very slowly the eyes looked at the reporter then closed halfway again and stayed there.

The cameraman was standing by the dead criminal's wife, conducting his own interview. "How do you feel now that your husband has been executed, ma'am?" he asked.

But what if the head was lying? This was a criminal, after all. What if it was nothing more than a bunch of nerve endings firing off without meaning anything? Go back to the science of physiognomy (about which 40 percent of the population says there is no such science, but 60 percent of the population knows someone or other who can "tell" when someone else is lying) and use its principles to decide whether the decapitated head was telling the truth when it fluttered its eyes.

Physiognomy says a glance to the right means an imaginative thought process. A glance to the left means a recall of memory.

The head glanced to the right. Now, if this were a poker game that would be considered a "tell" if the person did it autonomically in certain situations. Was this a "tell" from the dead head?

In other words, do the dead realize that their opinions still matter?

"Boss?" I asked politely. "Was that what you had in mind?"

"From now on," he said roughly. "No live segments. We're going to review your tapes and decide if they air."

"You didn't like it?" I was shocked.

"There are no guillotine executions in New Jersey," he said. "There never have been guillotine executions in New Jersey."

"Doesn't matter," I said. "The people still need to know."

According to a clairvoyant I consulted, the afterlife is just like this life, only without bodies. The poor are still poor, though this time they are also poor in spirit.

"How does that work?" I asked. "I mean, how can you be poor if there's no money?"

"Oh, there's money," she said. "It just doesn't weigh anything. Besides, *we* put the value on things. It's not like gold has any particular absolute value. We just like it. That's in this world," she said. "There are 10,000 worlds, but not really that much variety. Some are physical, some are spiritual. And they all have rich and poor people."

"What's the point?"

"No point. It simply is. Of course, you'll like it better if you're rich in all the worlds."

"So we *can* bring it with us?" I asked. "How do we prepare to be rich in the next life? Is there some kind of investment opportunity?"

I didn't believe her, of course; I could feel it creeping out of my voice. She was offended.

"You'll learn that your attitude always goes with you," she said stiffly.

I rapped on my table just for the effect. "I think I hear some advice," I said. "Do you know who it's from? I want to do a background check."

And she shut up. That was the end of the segment.

I wouldn't be surprised if there are scams beyond the grave. Some people will believe anything; other people will take advantage of anything.

So, beliefs. What are people willing to believe in? Some believe they have come from another planet; some believe they are going to one. Some believe they will gain their enemies' strengths by eating their enemies' hearts. Others try to claim the soul by, say, sprinkling water on the head or cutting off a bit of skin.

Almost everyone believes in some kind of conspiracy. Like my boss, I think he's working against me.

"You can make fun of the clairvoyants—hell, everyone makes fun of those. But what was that crack about stealing the soul? That was anti-religious. That kills ratings."

"Anti-religious?" I asked, aghast. "I just wanted to point out similarities, you know, parallels."

"Cannibalism and baptism?"

"I'm interested in the metaphysics."

"No."

"No?"

"We're not showing it."

We sat together in a companionable way. "Well, what *can* I cover? That has to do with metaphysics?"

"I don't even know what metaphysics is in this day and age," the boss muttered. "But you seem to like death. So I'm putting you in the morgue. Anytime someone dies, you write up the memorial and you find the clips."

"Let me think about it."

"That's really all there is," he said. "And you may have to do some typing besides."

I thought about it. I would still be on-camera, I could talk about the deaths of people who were either admirable or famous; I could wear dark colours, which I like very much. I could roam through photo morgues on company time. I could quote from poems about death. I could insist these dead people held interesting beliefs. Hell, everyone believes in something interesting sometime in their lives.

We need work, meaningful work, if we are to remake all 10,000 worlds. This is what I told the boss. "I'm yours," I said. "But give me a little latitude here. Let me ask how people feel about the death, whether it was the right thing or not."

"The right thing?" his mouth dropped open.

"Sometimes death is wrong," I said sternly.

He stared at me and sighed. "You can give me anything you want, as long as you cover their lifetimes. Do it that way: give me their lives, then give me their deaths."

I was very pleased. "I'll tell you what I think about your death right now," I said.

"No," he said. "I'd like to wait for that."

People once believed that the image of the murderer was etched on the retina of the victim's eyes, like a photographic plate. Like a little camera snapping its own evidence. It must have come from all that "eyes are the mirror of the soul" business. The mirror caught the last reflection and saved it.

No, wait. The eyes are the windows to the soul, I think. So what if it works the other way—the eyes record what the soul sees, it doesn't record what the body sees? No one ever found the murderer's image in the victim's eyes, but did they find something else? Did they see bits and pieces of things that made no sense? A line here, a curve there, none of which added up to anything individually? We are always leaving hieroglyphics, aren't we? Faery stiles, crop circles, Aztec ridges, Nazca lines. Little nicks on cave walls, rocks piled in patterns, dots and dashes. So why not messages for those left behind? It's hard to break that human compulsion to say one more thing.

What if there *are* imprints on the eyes of the dead after all, and they form a message when you put them all together? It's very exciting, when you see a puzzle for the first time; when you sense its solution. Human instinct; human intelligence; the human need to organize information and pass it on. What are polls for but to find the patterns we're secretly storing? What are books and films and TV shows and reports from all over the world except to find the pattern? Who says we would stop the trail, the interpretation, the insight, the comment, when all is said and done? Those who talk never stop talking. Those who reason never stop reasoning.

So I took the job. The boss said Morgues and I went to the morgues—not the library of clippings that he meant but the actual morgues. I spoke to the attendants, who told me that they kept music on to counter their fear of hearing whispers. They don't like the silence because it seems to be waiting. But then they laughed and they winked at each other.

I interviewed them myself and I taped them and I took their pictures. They want to believe they might be famous someday, though we never discussed for what.

"Boss, this is interesting," I said. "They dress the dead and take their pictures. They pose them. The families request it. The families of the long-lost ask to see them in a natural pose."

"Disgusting," he said. "Wait. Maybe an expose?"

But I won't expose them. The attendants let me in after hours. They don't say a word as I open the eyes of the dead and take their picture. I zoom in on the iris, on the retina, I snap them looking back at me on high-speed, on digital. I run home and I blow the photos up, looking for the shapes in the back of their eyes, the shapes that reflect something. Already I have pieced together, from selections of their eyes, the angle of a room, a white room with a doorway and a hall. The doorway has crystal doors, opened and not quite flat to the side. The hallway—I only see a little bit of the hallway and there is a shadow of a hand in it, just beyond the opened door. I can't see who is throwing that shadow. But I will find it out.

My walls are lined with rows and rows of these photos, the blown-up retinas of the dead. They all seem to be looking in the same direction. And in every one of them, there is a clue.

CREATING COW

"That one looks good," her mom said, rocking the plastic-wrapped package so that the juices flowed back and forth. It was bright red behind the plastic, cheery almost. Definitely looked clean. Pink and fresh and lovely.

Her mom put it in the cart. Doreen picked it up and poked it. "I wonder if it minds?" she asked, thinking out loud. This past year she had become unable to let go of connecting the meat to the animal. She kept picturing it, eyes wide with terror.

"It doesn't mind," her mom said soothingly. "Why would it mind?"

"Being killed. Getting sliced up. Wouldn't you mind?"

Her mom shrugged absently. "How about some potatoes? Or would you like noodles?"

"Do you think the other packages were the same cow? If I got the other packages, would it all fit back together again?" Doreen touched another package speculatively, testing it. She was seventeen, a senior in high school. She had refused to dissect a pig for Biology.

"Doreen, it's got nothing to do with you. That's what they're made for; that's what they want, really, when you think about it. Besides, it already happened, it's just meat now. You can't put it back together again like a jigsaw puzzle." Her mom's voice was soothing but automatic; she was used to Doreen's nonsense.

"I've heard people eat people," Doreen said thoughtfully, putting a fingertip on the package and poking it. "I wonder how they taste. What if that's really human meat?"

Her mom wheeled over to the produce department, pointing out fruit to her, covering up the meat with bananas and pears. "That will be lovely, won't it?" she asked. "Nice for dessert, with ice cream? Bananas and ice cream?" She had a great deal of hope in her voice.

At dinner she served the meat, covered in gravy, with mashed potatoes and peas. She snuck the meat under the mashed potatoes on Doreen's plate. She knew enough not to give her gravy, the girl was almost religious when it came to animals, but Doreen's father had gravy and he loved it. He looked away from her, mixing the stuff into his potatoes. Doreen wondered thoughtfully if cooking people made the same kind of gravy?

Doreen generally wore sneakers to school instead of leather shoes—cowskin shoes; she had told her mom last year that she would no longer wear animals. It was cold out and her gloves were good, microfiber. She kept the old leather gloves and the old leather shoes in her closet. She had looked at them last night, considering things. There were all these animal parts lying around, casually, innocently, and no one saw it but her. She was the kind of girl who saw patterns, and who tried to undo the bad patterns; she was the kind of girl who didn't pretend that today made yesterday irrelevant; she was the kind of girl who never doubted that unpleasant things should be changed.

At school her class was given mice for the year-end science project. The mice were going to be fed different fast-food items. Girls screamed at the mice and a boy picked one up and bit its tail off before anyone could do a thing. He grinned and looked around with the tail still twitching in his mouth. The teacher sent the boy (Wallace, a continuing problem when it came to small animals) to the principal, which didn't bother him in the least. A janitor came and took the mouse away and wiped up the mess. It would have been gravy if the mouse had been packaged, Doreen thought.

Doreen picked the mouse out of the garbage after school, waiting till everyone else went off racing, jumping and slapping each other. She always preferred to wait till the others were gone anyway and she knew better than to let anyone see her doing it. The mouse's head was bashed in, but she thought it might be useful, so she put it in her pocket. She had made a decision. It took a first step, weren't they always saying that? Someone had to stand up for the right thing, and she couldn't put it off any longer: she was that someone.

On the way home she stopped at the deli and bought five packages of cow. She was a little perplexed, since she wanted to get slices from the same cow. That way, when she put them all back together she wouldn't have to worry about rejection, which she had read about recently, when they had put a chimp heart into a man. They had showed the chimp being wheeled away, its hand outstretched.

She checked the date-stamp and divided the packages into piles, putting all the same dates together, and she took the pile with the most pieces. She put them in the cart, and the cashier laughed at her—a big eater? she asked—and double-bagged them so the blood wouldn't run out. Doreen watched her pat each one through the plastic. People were always patting meat.

The bag was heavy and dragged her down a little on one side, but she liked the weight of it; she had seen women carrying small dogs in carriers; perhaps that felt like this. When she passed another store she decided to go in just to check, and they had packages of cow too. Some of them had the same date as the ones she carried, and she thought this through. Sure, if they cut up the cow it would be all on the same day and then they'd send it around, so she bought all the packages that matched the date on the packages she already had. She was thinking of them as pieces of an animal she needed to rescue. She saw things that most other people did not; she made connections that other people ignored; she acted when others stood back.

She got the big sewing needle and thread her Mom used to sew the turkey shut with the stuffing inside it, making it neat and tidy, a process that appealed to Doreen. Making it whole and not empty; that must have given the turkey a sense of relief, if only for a while.

She knew she would have to keep the cow cold, so she began to sew it together in the garage. It was harder than she thought because only three pieces actually fit together with the same shape. She tried to settle on a way of putting the others together, moving them around and up and down and flipping them over, lots of various combinations, but she needed more shapes. She got paper and pen and outlined some of the pieces, and then she went to a larger supermarket, where she was sure there would be more date-stamped pieces. She had always been good with puzzles so there was a pleasure in strategizing.

It was bright and cheerful in the store. The refrigerated aisles hummed, the lights blinked. She passed by the ground meat—could that be something from her cow? Maybe those were the pieces that would have fit? She took out her tracings at the cut meats section and found three packages that might work, but she thought that the ground meat might be useful too, so she took two of those.

She got outside and then scooted around the back, passing the dumpster, where she found chicken feet and some wads of fat, like thick ribbons. And skin! It might have been pork skin, because it was pale, but all animals needed skin, so she rolled it up and put it in the bag, along with an expired fish and some turkey rolls.

It wasn't that hard, then, putting it all back together. Finding the pieces. She felt like she was doing a great good thing. Wherever the slices didn't come together, she put in some ground meat. In order to keep that from pushing out again, she got some gauze and put the gauze around the ground meat and then sewed that to the firm meats. She wrapped skin at the joints and patted it all together gently, as if she were petting a dog or primping hair. She said little words occasionally, to encourage it.

She didn't know whether it was a he or a she, because she had to take different parts as she needed them from different things. There was the pork skin, yes, and she was inclined to think of it as a he, but as she put the meats together she realized she needed to support it, and so she got some bones ("for a very large dog") from the butcher. The cow was really a mixed cow.

It had a shape, kind of. It sort of stood up and hunched over. It had patches of hair on its lumpy head. When it oozed, she used plastic wrap to keep it firm.

It had a mouth. She had found a tongue, set on a foam plate and sealed and dated. She had made lips from the gloves. She'd put in marbles for teeth, then replaced them as she found false teeth in a dentist's garbage bin. She looked for the scarlet bags of medical waste around the clinics late at night and she pulled out a thumb. She had heard in school that what made humans rank high above the animals was an opposable thumb. She wanted the animal to rank high.

She gave it two hearts, still in their plastic sacks. She found a brain and put it behind its fish eyes. And finally she thought it might be ready. She took it out of the cold and let it warm up, braised it with chicken stock, beef stock, minerals and herbs, stood it in a pan of stock, let it absorb some of the vitality, waited and stepped back. She threw in some Echinacea. Maybe an electric shock? An electric shock then, a curling iron turned on and sunk into the stock.

Phffft! The meat jolted upright. Should she do it again? Then it opened its mouth and screamed.

Slaughterhouse scream. Horrible.

It staggered around, lifting its head again, screaming. Doreen, heart pounding, threw juices at it, because it banged around like it was burning, and the juices seemed to help. Not enough skin? She threw all the juices and it stood there quivering, so she got plastic wrap and wrapped it tight around it.

She had given it eyes, and the eyes gazed at her. Its mouth rippled, trying to find a form.

It screamed again, but this time not so hard, and Doreen stood, watching it. There was an answering chorus of barks and some howls from far off.

There had been piglets at a petting zoo she'd once been taken to. "Don't name them," her father had said. "You've got to understand they're food, not pets."

"Your name is Gilgamesh," Doreen said. It was a name they'd read about in school and she liked the sound of it, exotic and strong. And wasn't Gilgamesh a king of some sort?

Gilgamesh opened his mouth, rolled his eyes, and shifted his head. He moved his arms and then his torso. The suede of his lips parted and came together. He looked at his arms, which ended bluntly, and lifted what should be his hands. Or cow feet. Or paws.

Doreen nodded. "I couldn't find any hands, just that thumb. I suppose they were eaten," she said. "I tried to find what I could."

With that, the cow struck at her, hitting her with the meat on its paw, or hand. She was flung back. "But I saved you!" she cried out.

Gilgamesh mooed, or hooted, a long loud call. The dogs all barked in answer. Doreen thought she heard birds as well, those loud pushy ones, the crows.

There was no expression on Gilgamesh's face—for she hadn't given him delicate muscles. He lifted his arm again, brought it back, and knocked Doreen to the ground. Then he rushed away. Doreen rolled over, getting her breath back, dizzy. Her hand braced itself on the floor, in some of the blood that Gilgamesh had dripped.

No, actually it was her own blood; her nose was bleeding. She sat back, thickheaded.

She heard yells from the houses around them, and her mother called out, asking what was wrong. Dogs barked in excitement. She got up and followed the sounds, yelling back to her mother that everything was fine, determined to make sense of what was happening. She could fix it, she was sure, if she could understand it.

Gilgamesh was roaming the neighbourhood, smashing into things, calling out wildly, and the neighbourhood animals answered. Tied up, fenced in, they howled to him, flinging themselves against walls and trees and cages. Doreen followed the noises of people shouting, but there was a panic in the street, and people ran every which way, so she wasn't sure of the direction.

Her mother stood on the steps waiting for her. "What is it?" she asked. "I've heard terrible things. There's a news report about wild dogs. Did you see them?"

Doreen shook her head. "They're not wild, they're just running."

"Come inside, Doreen, it isn't safe. What if they start biting people? Biting children? We can't have that." The sounds were far off now, going away fast. Doreen hesitated and then went inside.

That night the news reports showed police on top of buildings and crouching through alleyways. They said they would shoot any animal that ran past. The reporter showed gates that had been broken in certain yards where "a thing" had stumbled through.

"This is terrible," her mother said. "What's going on, who let that thing out? I won't rest until it's dead, whatever it is."

"It's probably just unhappy," Doreen said stubbornly.

She waited for her parents to fall asleep. Then she dressed and snuck outside. She took a packet of instant gravy with her, just in case.

The streets were flooded with flashing lights, so she took the back yards, sneaking through bushes and behind sheds, falling over bicycles and mowers. She followed her own old routes, going behind the butchers, the stores, the dog pounds, the vet. She found Gilgamesh near the dumpsters behind the biggest supermarket, surrounded by dogs.

"You can't stay here," she said. "They're looking for you. They want to kill you."

Gilgamesh had a piece of meat hanging off near his shoulder and she went up to him very carefully. She wanted to put it back in place, but she didn't have a needle and thread. She should have thought of that; she really should have.

"They're killing other animals because of you," she said unhappily. Gilgamesh lowered his great uneven head. "More and more. It's my fault. I didn't think about this too clearly. It just seemed so wrong, and yet this isn't any better. I don't know what to do." She thought it would be best if Gilgamesh just went away, far away, so that all of this could stop—the shooting that she heard, even now, blocks away, the cries of an animal being hit, of people being excited. Yet she felt sad for Gilgamesh, too; for he now had a voice and an intent. Why else would he be roaming the streets? Why else was he learning to live?

Doreen ripped open her packet of gravy and sprinkled it on his shoulder, pinching the pieces together. It didn't fully stick together, but it was better. "You have to get away from here," she said, and led him past the dumpsters to the industrial park, and beyond that to the woods. Maybe he would be safe there. And if the animals followed him, maybe the shooting would stop. He loped along, shifting from side to side, his gait worse than it had been earlier that day. She frowned, trying to see what was wrong. Some of his body had slid down farther, she thought, so that his weight dragged down to his legs.

She lay in bed that night, listening to the guns and the shouts and the drawn out animal screams. She had an awful feeling that she'd done the wrong thing, that Gilgamesh was a mistake, but how could that be? And if he was, what could she do?

In the morning she went out again and searched for him, back up in the woods, hoping she'd find him and that she would somehow know what the right thing to do would be. There was a sweet smell in the air, but it wasn't a nice smell. It made her slow down a little, but it didn't stop her entirely. Perhaps he was dead already; that would be the easiest thing.

A dog walked with her, a little bit away, its tail held high, its mouth open eagerly. She followed the dog and found Gilgamesh leaning against a large tree. His head was sloping downwards and to the side, and she could see that a piece of his back leg had fallen off. Some dogs were fighting over something in the bushes.

Gilgamesh lifted his injured leg when she approached him. He tried to straighten up. The dog walked over and began to lick at Gilgamesh's feet. "Stop it!" she cried and threw a stick at the dog, who went away and sat down, watching.

She didn't want him to die. He had a right to live—

she had, she thought, given him the right to live. She'd brought water and thread and some more plastic wrap, but his meat came apart easily and it was impossible to get it all to stay together. She thought she might be able to go and find more meat, fresher packages, a later sell-by date, maybe she could still fix him. But it struck her that it was wrong to use the meat of other animals to keep him alive. It was contrary to what she had wanted, wasn't it? Every time she remembered this it sent a little shock of despair right through her.

His skin was too soft, and parts of it were dried at the edges. "Wait," she said, and she ran back to the store, looking for beef stock, chicken stock, even vegetable stock. "My, my," the cashier said. "Soup? Looks like a lot of soup." And the cashier smiled happily, a soup-lover herself.

She dribbled the broth over him slowly; she rubbed it in around his head, massaging his neck and his forehead. When he was stronger, she tugged him gently deeper into the woods, away from the people who wanted to catch him. She threw stones at the dogs, scattering them. Then she rushed home, telling her mother she'd been right next door, out of harm's way. Her mother frowned and looked at her sharply, but let it go.

Doreen rose before dawn and found Gilgamesh and led him to the garbage cans on the street, opening up the plastic wraps and the brown paper bags, searching for discarded meats—old chops, dry slices of turkey, oozing packages of bacon. Gilgamesh bent over them, tilting his head so that his fish eye could see. His hand with the thumb reached out and took a slice of meat and folded it into his lower leg, pressing it in. A bag of dented cans burst open and he picked up soups and gravies, scooping out the remnants and applying them to the slice of meat around the edges, making sure it was firmly in place.

She put the garbage back in the bin and they continued. She could see that Gilgamesh was intent on exploring each trash can and by the third or fourth he was selective and much quieter. She took out a plastic bag that was in good shape and put some things in it and he did so as well, picking out tuna salad, hamburgers, the gristle off steaks, chicken bones and shrimp tails. He loped along, an odd shambling walk, evidence of her lack of skill. With the bulging plastic bag he seemed an odd, unbalanced imitation cow or horse, or even a bear. Not well-defined, certainly. But alive, most definitely.

She led him back to the spot in the woods she had chosen. Then she hurried home and crept into bed.

She found him again the next day at dawn and he was greedier at the garbage cans, faster, ripping through bags impatiently, finding lard and chicken fat and drippings in plastic containers, congealed stews and overcooked fish. She followed him, trying to pick up the garbage he discarded, but she couldn't get it all done by dawn, he worked so furiously. She had worn sneakers and running clothes in case her mother got up before she got home, but she crept inside unobserved.

She took out their own garbage that night, keeping herself from sorting it only by an enormous effort.

"Make sure the lid is on tight," her mother warned. "It's raccoons. All that fuss. Raccoons. They went through every garbage can on Kessel Street," she said. "*Monsters*, ha! Some people have active imaginations. Just make sure the lid's on tight."

She worked harder at cleaning up behind Gilgamesh, but there was never enough time; he went from can to can recklessly, gathering meats and liquids. He didn't always wait for her, and she had to come earlier, hours before dawn, to catch him.

And then he moved. She stood at his usual spot, shining her flashlight around, afraid that something terrible had happened. She saw a trail of flattened ferns and followed it, her heart pounding, looking at shapes quickly and then away and then back at them again.

Finally her light flashed on him. His back was turned from her. She called out and he stiffened, then moved to look at her, his thick arms dragging. His body was heavy and loose. She could see bits of garbage around him, foam plates, plastic wrap. She wondered if he had a need to repair himself in privacy. Some animal instinct to conceal his weakness, maybe? She turned slightly away from him, to protect his feelings.

When he was ready, she took him to a mini-mall with a specialty shop, and Gilgamesh found dented cans of consommé, dirty cans of oxtail soup in addition to dried-out ends of deli meats. She had brought a cloth bag to make it easier for Gilgamesh to carry his finds. She made him close the lid on the dumpster and had him repeat the action until she was sure he understood. It was light; she began to hear cars on the avenue, so she hurried him back into the woods. Gilgamesh was even clumsier than usual, pushing roughly through the bushes and undergrowth, moving hastily to his new area, where two small bush trees, their lower branches broken, formed a kind of cave. Gilgamesh headed to it directly, his back to Doreen, filling the space quickly so that all she glimpsed was a mound of leaves. His hand must have brushed the leaves because for a second she thought she saw a movement. She was tired and it was just before dawn; no doubt she had imagined it.

Her mother asked her if she was sick when she overslept, and Doreen was careful for the next few days to keep to a normal schedule. That weekend she snuck out again, worried how Gilgamesh was doing. The blue pre-dawn made Kessel St., normally so orderly and self-conscious, seem gloomy. The only oddity on the street was a flyer on a lamppost, advertising a lost dog. On the next street she saw one for a lost cat, and Doreen began to feel a sense of alarm. But there could hardly be a connection, she told herself. The memory, though, of Gilgamesh hunkering down over something that was now, in her mind, most definitely moving—it horrified her. Why hadn't she looked?

She found Gilgamesh in his green cave, his back resting against the tree trunk behind him, his right arm flung out, his left arm hugging something to his side, and Doreen felt her dread increase as she crept closer. She wanted it not to be a small dead animal he clutched; she wanted to believe that her fears were unfounded; she wanted to believe he was still innocent.

He lifted his head and saw her just as she saw what he held.

Gilgamesh's arm surrounded a smaller version of himself, even more awkwardly constructed and held together with tape and the small coated ties that held sandwich bags together. Gilgamesh rolled his great fish eye to her and then back to his makeshift child and then, in a gesture of trust that tore at Doreen's heart, he put the child on the ground, where it wobbled tentatively before taking a step towards her.

She could see that the lips and arms were stubs, and would need new attachments, new meats to stabilize it. But the face, she noticed, was quite good, much better than she had done, skillful.

It blinked at her and then she realized that the eyes were mammal eyes, not fish eyes. She stiffened in concentration, dreading to notice more details, but helpless against her own desire to know. *Cat's eyes.*

"Gilgamesh," she said finally. "No. You cannot kill things. No killing," she said feebly as Gilgamesh turned his head from her to the stubby creature on the ground. "Let's go," she said uncertainly. But Gilgamesh sat, his gaze on his child, and Doreen thought it would be best after all, if she gathered scraps of food for him. For them.

She went farther away so as not to empty out the sources nearest to Gilgamesh's cave; she wanted him to find food easily, not be tempted to go after any other pets. She wondered how he caught them, though, how he killed them. Pets on chains; pets in dog houses; cats asleep in the sun?

She brought back bags and bags of discarded foods, dripping pink spots along the street until she noticed and tried to restrict her steps to lawns and dirt. She ran home, later than usual, reeking of garbage, and met her mother at the door.

"Have you been out all night?" Her mother stood there, coffee in hand, judgemental, her nose sniffing. "And what's that smell? Are you drunk?"

Hastily, Doreen said she'd gone out for a run and slipped on some spilled garbage. Her mother weighed her words and scanned the stains on her arms. "That's blood," she said, surprised. "What's that blood from?"

Doreen felt an impulse to tell her mother everything—it was lonely having so much knowledge—but she pulled herself back. Who would look at Gilgamesh and let him live? Her mother's world was orderly, and Gilgamesh was not. "It must have been in the garbage," Doreen said wearily, and went to shower.

Her mother's eye was always on her then, checking her comings and goings, studying her clothes. When Doreen went to find Gilgamesh, he had moved, and she couldn't find a new trail to him.

More pets went missing; more flyers appeared. And then finally someone managed to take a picture of forms moving through the woods. There were three of them now, and their movements were smoother; she could imagine them sneaking up on pets and reaching out with a quick, meaty grab.

The notices were everywhere, for disappearing cats and dogs and once for a picnic cooler; suddenly people were posting all the things they suspected they'd lost. A few took guns and went into the woods; the only one who didn't make it back was thought to have deserted his family—the neighbourhood had been watching him for years and knew he was just the type to take advantage of any excuse to disappear. He was not a casualty but an opportunist.

Doreen walked home from school and saw toddlers in yards, saw babies in prams snoozing on front porches. She saw open windows in the evening, with stuffed toys lined up on the sill. She couldn't find Gilgamesh and she didn't know how to stop him.

She thought of Gilgamesh out there, somewhere, and the community he was creating. It was a difficult thing, feeling responsible for a creature so dangerous; at least that's what she usually thought. But sometimes she felt bigger, stronger, for having done it, for knowing she'd done it.

At night she slipped out now, through the darkness, putting up posters of her own. "Watch your children," the posters said. "He's coming."

She was a child herself. Maybe he would find her.

BEDS

There are twelve beds in the hospital ward today; tomorrow there will be eleven.

My right-hand bedmate is instantly conciliatory to the hospital staff: "Of course you are overburdened," she says, her voice dripping with compassion, "and there is at least one person here who is creating his own disease, just for attention. At least one," she says, and shuts up, her hands placed saintly on the top bed sheet.

"Is that me? Is that who you mean?" This comes from the end of the row against the wall, at the end of the line. "I have been dragged about by life—do you think you can be dragged all over the place without being wounded? That life doesn't wound you? That life doesn't kill you? There's no worse thing than that. I ask you," he said, pointing to the nurse with her cart of medications. "Do you have a cure for life?"

"Oh, we all get cured of *that* eventually," the nurse said, largely ignoring him and moving on. "I want to watch you take that, now," she said severely to the skinny man past the conciliatory woman, who took it glumly and popped it in but didn't swallow. "It could be you on that bed tomorrow, dearie. Is that what you want?"

He swallowed hastily and she put a tick on the chart on her clipboard.

"Where's the bed going?" I asked. They all had such narrow concerns; their fear overruled their curiosity. One bed less, one patient less; what did it matter? I was feverish and wobbly; they would let me stay. Surely. Neither the healthiest nor the sickest. Safe.

She handed me three pills and a pink liquid, and never looked to see if I took any of it. Was that a good sign?

"This one over here," the bed opposite me said. She was younger than most of us, and she often had cheery people tromping in and out. "With the annoying voice. Get rid of that one." I gloated over her spitefulness. Young and spiteful! Let her be the one.

"Don't you think I know about my voice?" the accused woman said. "Isn't that why I'm here? I will do anything, suffer anything to fix it, this curse of mine. I know how irritating my voice is, I hear about it over and over; I see how people turn away. I cringe when I speak," she said, closing her eyes and bringing her hand up to her throat. "How I detest it. Imagine—hating it and unable to stop it. It is a terrible fate. Terrible, terrible."

"The least you can do is stop talking about it so much," her tormentor said. "Like some electronic screech, you should really start using a pen and a pad. Give us all some relief."

"And you think I don't suffer?" the horrible voice asked. "To see how people react, to hear how you insult me: do you think I am heartless, soulless, without feelings, cursed as I am with a voice that doesn't suit me, doesn't match me—"

"Oh, it matches you, all right. You are not a quiet person; try being a quiet person."

"Oh? I'm the only one who should be silent? I suffer just to please everyone, I'm to be cut open from nose to throat, all to please you, and people like you, and never to speak?"

"That would be lovely."

"Well, let me tell you—" she began, but the nurse with her cart handed her a raft of pills, and she began to swallow them.

In the bed to her left a businesslike man said, "And who judges which bed goes? And when will this take place? And where does the bed go? Will it be the sickest or the least sick? Or," and here he shot a look at the woman with the awful voice, "the most annoying?"

"The doctors will decide," the nurse said indifferently. "They have been trained for it, and as to where the bed goes—why, it goes on a truck and we never ask where. Once you leave, you know, you don't exist for us. We are busy enough as it is, constantly reading your charts and discussing your medications and seeing who is doing well and who is not—"

"I want to do well," the thin man said. "I concentrate every day on a healthy attitude—"

"Which I take to mean that it is your *attitude* that will cure you and not the medical profession?" the nurse asked darkly.

He realized his error and produced a sticky grin, saying, "Of course not—very much appreciated," and flattened himself out against the sheets.

All the patients had their pills by now and they shifted, awaiting effects and peering glumly at the doorway.

Evening rounds: surely there would be evening rounds? And would it be decided then?

"My brother-in-law knows the head of the hospital," my neighbour whispered. "It won't be me, I can tell you. I hate the man, but he has his uses."

And I thought: I know no one. It felt electrical at first and then the stab of it broke off in a kind of dreadful flutter of the gut. I threw my eyes around the room, and I began to see their criteria in different terms: not the sickest or the healthiest, but the one most likely to leave no ripple behind, their disappearance unremarked, even satisfying, acknowledging an utter uselessness. There is one like that in every room, in every plot, in every family—the one who won't be missed, who stands at the back in photographs, or perhaps only a hand is seen, thrust from the outside of the group, or who is turned away, always turned away, when everyone else is gazing forward.

I was torn from my reveries, hearing my own name called, and indeed it was the lead doctor, head of the ward, standing at the foot of my bed, radiating certitude. She smiled at me, assertive in her white coat, her white bright hands, the preparation of her words jostling toward her tongue.

"Enough!" I cried before she could speak my name again, and I sat up and then stood, panting until the room steadied and the multitude of faces settled back to the eleven others, and I saw the nurse departing, and the doctor watching me with a bored clinical eye. "It is enough!" I cried again and I took the cloth jacket neatly folded out of my bedside table, and the shoes from their plastic case. "Don't speak my name," I shouted to the doctor and I turned to the beds and said, "I know you think it should be me—I know in the back of your heads you said, of course it must be that one, and I'll throw it back at you, then: Of course it's me! But I shall walk away from you, not be rowed away to Lethe on a bed. Cowards! You force me to it because I can see how vile are your fears, your contempt, yet they only give me vigour! I'll go, then, I'll set you free, you worthless dregs, you broken toys!" And I began feebly to make my way to the corridor.

"Now hold on," said the doctor. "I merely meant to compliment you on how well you're doing. Quiet, uncomplaining—though we'll have to make a note now, won't we?" She turned to face the centre of the room as, with a sigh of relief mixed with disappointment, I removed my coat, my shoes, and inserted myself back into bed. The doctor went to stand at the foot of the bed of the thinnest man, the man who had to be watched to swallow his pills.

The doctor lowered her voice, though we all heard it still and it thrilled us. "You, Hanley, it is your bed that we have chosen."

"Ah no!" he cried, pulling the sheets up to his chin, his eyes wide and unreflecting.

A cheerful buzz rose from the other patients. "I apologize," I said, "it was the fever that did it to me, for I have loved you all as brothers, sisters, hating you sometimes, it's true, but only as one hates within a family, intimately—all save Hanley, who doesn't provoke me at all."

"All save Hanley!" responded the other beds, as the orderlies came and pushed him away. He clutched the hem of his sheet, his lips quivering, his thin head with its pointed bones swivelling to gaze at each of us in turn. He may have said something—in fact, I'm sure he said something—but it was feeble and lost in the murmurs that rose up once his bed rounded the doorway and faded into the corridor.

"How odd," said my neighbour to the left, "but I feel—suddenly—finer. I can think clearly, I'm sure of it."

"That pounding in my chest is gone," another declared.

"Do you know—I think I'm hungry."

And we all had grins on our faces at the prospect of returning health. Was it coincidence that it had to do with Hanley's removal? Was it an accident that once he left we all felt better?

Hanley was the cause of all our distress, and without him, we agreed, our lives were sure to be long and safe. "We will live," we murmured to each other, "we are whole; it was Hanley all along!" And we blessed our doctors and our nurses and the orderlies who took Hanley from us, the creature who would blacken our hearts.

HOW LIGHTLY HE STEPPED IN THE AIR

Sam himself was probably the last one to realize it.

"Have you noticed anything about Sam lately?" Dolores asked Don. They had adjoining desks. Sam had just passed by.

Don shrugged and his glasses slipped down his nose. "Nothing, no. What do you mean?"

Dolores turned to Betty on her other side. The desks were arranged in rows. "Have you noticed?"

"Too busy," Betty said. "I never notice walks anyway."

"Still," Dolores said dreamily, "still, there's something . . ."

Sam had not yet noted the change in his walk. He did, however, feel a certain pleasant lightness.

He had gotten as far as the designers' offices when a surprised voice said, "How did you do that?"

Sam had not done anything. He had merely stepped over a wadded piece of paper on the carpeted floor. "Do what?"

"You stepped over the paper, but you didn't—well—

land right away. Is it a trick?" the woman, whose name Sam did not know, looked at him with admiration.

"No trick at all," Sam said, smiling with his broken tooth showing. He walked on, with that new, light tread Dolores had mentioned, thinking only that the woman was flirting. Sam, at the moment, felt above flirting. But the woman's suggestion remained in the back of his mind.

For instance, it was only a day or so later that he reached for a particular book awkwardly placed a little too high on a shelf above his drafting table. He was surprised to find that he had left the ground. "Odd," he remarked as he gently regained the floor. And then he laughed at himself. What a silly thought to have! He laughed again.

But Dolores, having happened to glance up from the row of desks where she worked across to the row of drafting tables where Sam worked, leaned over and nudged Don.

"I just saw him do it again."

"I won't believe it till I see it myself," Don muttered in irritation. "You *say* you see it, but no one else does."

"Well, then, *watch*," she hissed back.

Don lifted his chin haughtily. "I'm busy. I'm working."

"I do the same work you do, and get it done in the same amount of time, and yet I can still manage to keep in touch with the world around me."

Don did not even condescend to sniff in response, but Betty, on Dolores's other side, said, "You know, it's funny, but I could almost swear . . ." She stopped uncertainly.

Sam sat thoughtfully in front of his draft board. He was no longer chuckling. That feeling of lightness he had—was it more than a feeling? He chewed thoughtfully on his moustache. Had he really learned a trick of some kind?

Once conscious of his new skill, Sam began to notice it more and more. He lived in a fourth-floor walk-up and it finally dawned on him, on the way home, how easy the stairs had become lately. In fact, once started, he drifted up effortlessly.

The next morning, coming downstairs began to be more of an effort. He had to grasp the handrail—gently, it's true—to pull himself gradually down. Otherwise he moved very markedly forward, rather than down.

Sam began, tentatively, to test himself. Dolores was on the alert, and was able to nudge Don in time for him to see Sam as he took a gentle leap up to the top row of shelves and hovered there considering titles.

Don did not give in easily. "It's a trick of some kind."

"But what a trick!" Dolores breathed.

Sam exhaled and descended gently to the floor. Pencil in hand, he doodled rather than drafted at his board. If it was true, if it was really true . . . was it possible to put this to use somehow? His mind wandered.

Word spread along the rows of desks and drafting tables. Sam's neighbours, hunched over their boards, had noticed nothing, but once alerted by Dolores, everyone kept an eye, or corner of an eye, watchfully on him.

Sam drifted by them, more obviously, day by day, floating.

There were various explanations.

"Maybe it's glandular."

Don was not to be appeased. "He's just doing it to get attention."

"Is he an air sign?"

"No, he's a Pisces."

"Well, fish float."

Out of curiosity, people along the rows set traps for him. Suddenly there would be wastepaper baskets, cartons, or even chairs left temptingly in between the rows, directly in Sam's path.

Sam was feeling lighter and lighter. He smiled as he stepped widely, gently, tenderly above cartons and chairs. The uninitiated would get a nod from those now familiar with Sam's floating.

Everyone had some comment to make. Sam now spent little time on the ground.

"He'd make a great second-story man," someone said speculatively.

But Sam had not figured out any use for floating, and it no longer mattered to him. He was happy to float. He began to do it in public—on street corners, in subways.

The urge would overcome him. He would smile, a small smile at first and then more expansive. He always had to step in order to rise; he couldn't do it sitting down.

First the smile, then a lighthearted step and that wonderful lift into the air. He hung there—oh, what did the length of time matter, except that it increased subtly day by day?

People began to notice him on the street. If he jumped a curb, almost certainly someone would say, "Oh, look, that's the same one we saw yesterday." And maybe there would be the answer, "Oh, no, I think that one had a beard. Still, it might be the same."

Sam's smile, then, became almost beatific. Where he had loomed previously only a head above the crowd he now appeared head and shoulders.

The gradual settling down to Earth had a calming effect on him; it soothed him after the euphoria of his float.

Dolores once asked him—for she never questioned his ability, or thought it a trick—whether it was like certain dreams she'd had.

"It's not at all like a flying dream," he answered. "Unless you have flying dreams where you stand up? In that case it might be." Sam had ceased to dream, anyway. He also couldn't recall any of his old dreams. Apparently, he no longer needed them.

Sam's reputation in the office was spreading. The rows where he worked were now very often cluttered with people who had no particular business being there, who "just stopped by" to say hello to an unnamed acquaintance.

This caused Don, who resented the attention paid to such an extraordinarily shallow form of amusement, a great deal of bitterness.

"He's just doing it for effect," he told Dolores and Betty more than once. "He thinks he's special."

"He is special," Dolores repeated.

"Let's just say 'boo' when he doesn't expect it, and see what happens," Betty whispered, raising her eyebrows.

"That'll just encourage him," Don sniffed. He shuffled the papers on his desk in disapproval.

Sam began to have difficulty getting back down to the ground. He was perplexed by this. When he took an elevator he continued to rise after the doors opened. People sometimes had to pull him down, like the pulling, they told him, of a large helium-filled balloon.

Although he could relax sitting down, he did not

necessarily rest on the chair. He began to suspect that he was actually beginning to float in any position—but not at all times, perhaps only when his mind wandered and he thought about his mysterious gift.

He told Dolores he'd been to a fortune-teller. She had discussed only his present and past and vigorously shook her head when asked about his future.

Sam fingered his moustache sadly and settled only a few inches above the ground. "It's the not having a future that seems surprising."

"A man who can *fly*," Dolores said. "How can there be a predictable future? Wind currents alone . . ."

Sam stopped her with a gesture. "It hasn't gotten that bad yet."

"Ah, but, as you said, she couldn't see the future."

Sam gradually settled a few inches higher. That very morning he had woken with his nose smack against the ceiling.

In fact, Sam was afraid he was losing all control over his gift. Crowds collected around him almost constantly now, since he rose so consistently and conspicuously at every opportunity. It was all right now, in the summer, to hover giddily in the air until it was time to come down to Earth—but in winter? In winter it could be unpleasant, at the rate he was going, to be stranded outside a third-story office window waiting for whatever it was that took him down again.

And it might not even wait till winter. At the rate he was going, by the time the leaves fell off the trees he would be evaporating into the stratosphere. How high, indeed, would he go? Was there a limit to his powers—or none at all?

His work was suffering, he had to admit. It was difficult enough trying to stay in some sort of relative proximity to his table, but his mind wandered so often (and as his mind wandered, so did his body) that he spent whole hours in idle trains of thought. The designs he handed in were incomplete, or they had certain erratic elements incorporated into them that caused consternation in the upper ranks.

The floor manager had spoken to him already a few times—at first tentatively, because he liked Sam. But he had been getting words, stronger and stronger, from those above. His heart thudded every time he saw Sam sitting in the air above his table, abstractedly staring into the distance. Sam was becoming a continuing disturbance, and disturbances did not help productivity.

The manager, Peter, overheard parts of the many conversations about Sam. He knew, for example, how irritated Don was with Sam's unprofessional stance. And Don was the kind of person capable of making his complaints known straight up and down the hierarchy—even over Peter's head. Peter also knew about the minor betting that was going on about the time and height of Sam's best levitation each day—had even participated, much earlier on, with his own crumpled dollar.

But the encouragement—the egging on—that now continually interrupted the workday was beyond his tolerance and even beyond his specific orders.

Still, he could hear Don vexedly saying, "Oh, don't ask him to do that, we'll *never* hear the end of it," and knew that his staff had come up with yet another test or trial for Sam to perform.

Dolores's voice answered back, "Oh, but we have to

see just what he can do. He doesn't know it himself. In the interests of science!" She laughed gaily; she had begun to feel that Sam was her property, her discovery. Peter shuddered and turned away. Perhaps the situation could be covered by a memo. He rapidly composed it as he hurried down the corridor. "To all staff members: In the interests of professionalism, only those authorized to be in the Design Department will be admitted during their normal shifts. We would also like to point out that betting pools of any kind are strictly prohibited, and this prohibition will be enforced. In addition, business hours do not include the performance of any tricks or attention-gathering activities that distract from a working environment." Yes, he thought, something along those lines would be appropriate.

Sam found that putting weights in his shoes did not work. He contrived to belt himself into the chair at work, but that began to drift with him as well. He requested metal bolts to keep his chair connected to the floor and Peter agreed to it. Sam rigged up all manner of devices to make it possible to stay strapped into his chair and still reach the materials he needed to work with.

But when he had to leave his chair the office effectively stopped working and a pleasant thrill of expectation spread down the rows. Sam now had gotten into the habit of holding onto the corners of desks and chairs as he walked down the aisle, as an astronaut might grope his way through space.

His smile had a worried edge to it. He became afraid of open spaces—areas without handles, or bars, or mailboxes to grab when the push upward became imperative.

His power, or gift, or trick, or curse, was escalating. He was almost never on the ground. And it had lost its interest for him; now that it was no longer a plaything, he was becoming more aware of the disadvantages. He regretted what he had said to Dolores (how recently was it?): "Sometimes I wonder how high I can go. I am the first."

When he went for a drink of water and ended up standing above the water cooler, he was no longer curious about floating; it was no longer theoretical. He faced a practical problem. If he lost this job, he would have a particularly difficult time at job interviews. He twisted his mouth painfully at the thought.

But then there came a day when the straps of his chair no longer held him. They burst, not forcefully, but almost without comment, and Sam did not reach out quickly enough to hold himself down.

Unfortunately, it happened while a top executive was leading a tour through the building. They had been marching all morning up one aisle, one corridor after another, nodding and gravely paying attention to various aspects of dynamic management, theoretical projection and design. Sam, as a member of the Design Department, was on the last leg of the tour. The top executive was proud of this section—the rows of desks and draft boards were not the head or heart of the organization, but their sheer extent was impressive.

Unfortunately, Sam was by then firmly resting against the ceiling, and at least a dozen people who should have been at their desks were trying to get him down.

The tour stopped short at this crowd, and a horrible quiet descended along the rows. Everything stopped. All eyes and ears were turned in one direction.

"Peter," the top executive said to the manager, "is there an explanation for this?"

Peter was in misery. After all, he *liked* Sam. But to be put in such a position!

"He floats," was Peter's strangled reply.

The executive regarded the situation with a cold, slow eye. He glanced from Sam on the ceiling, to the people stopped in their attempt to pull him down, to the unpleasantly meaningful quiet of the multitude of workers around them.

His slow survey seemed interminably long. Finally he said, "I'll drag him down to Earth. He's fired."

And with a very deliberate, self-conscious tread, he led his tour back through the aisles, as with very deliberate, self-conscious movements, workers along the rows bent down their heads and gave at least a pretense of busyness.

Sam heard it with a sinking heart (if anything about him were capable of sinking) and was forced to wait until the very bravest souls got him down from the ceiling.

"You'll get severance pay," Peter told him as he circled unhappily. "And use me as a reference. If only you would stop *floating*." He gave it a particularly vehement emphasis.

"I don't care!" Dolores cried. "It's wonderful that he can do it! And it's wrong to fire him!"

"It's out of my hands now," Peter sighed.

Sam nodded unhappily, gripping his chair. "And out of mine, too," he said. He felt terrible; it must be what alcoholics feel when they realize they have, finally, lost everything of value. What was to become of him? He felt the powerful pull upwards, and tightened his grip on the chair.

"Someone has to help me," he said sadly. "I'll be back on the ceiling again."

"Here, you," Peter called out, embarrassed and upset. "You there—grab his arm." He gestured as two men stepped forward and held onto Sam. "What else can I do, Sam?"

Sam drifted slightly in the air. "No, there's nothing else."

They pulled him through the aisles to the front door. Peter and Dolores followed.

Outside, they hesitated uncertainly. "I have to leave you here," Peter said finally. "I have to go back or there will be more trouble." He turned to go, and then his eyes fell on the men holding Sam down. "They have to get back to work, too, Sam."

One man let go and Sam began to rise when he cried out suddenly, "Not yet!" The man grabbed hold again and they all looked silently at Sam.

"I don't know what it is," Sam said huskily, gulping air, "but I don't want to let go now."

"But Sam, think of it!" Dolores begged.

"The sky looks so empty. And huge." He sighed, and that shifted him slightly so he was harder to hold.

He bobbed gently. "Not now. Not yet."

Peter eyed him with a worried frown. "There's a rope inside," he said without emphasis, and Sam answered, "A rope would be good." A breeze caused him to pull gently away and then bump back against the men who held him.

Peter wound one end of the rope around Sam's waist and over both his shoulders in a kind of harness. They all found it easier to control Sam if they let him rise four or five feet above the ground.

"That's all we can do, Sam," Peter said nervously. "We have to go back."

"Tie me to that tree," he said. "Just for a while."

Peter and Dolores huddled in brief conferences during the rest of the afternoon. He looked worried; she looked sad. Betty walked down the corridors to the front door. "Leg cramps," she said to Peter. She confirmed that Sam was still there.

Dolores left work early, as did the two men who had held onto Sam before. They got a cab, hauled Sam down and pushed him into it.

Dolores believed that eventually Sam would be free, that it was only a small matter of time before the sky looked more comforting, before he felt the final pull of invisible wings. She wanted to see it; she believed it so fiercely.

"A little longer," Sam said, as he drifted outside her windows, tethered to the large tree in her backyard, looming and disappearing, turning as the breezes turned him, his eyes stoically forward, his face composed in a pleasant but uncommitted smile, the ropes around him each day more taut and straining, his hands locked together and reaching downward, toward where he wanted to be, on the Earth.

THE DIFFICULTIES OF EVOLUTION

"I want to save this one," Franka said, stroking Yagel, her youngest. The child sat in Franka's lap, her dark eyes following the doctor happily. She chattered and waved her small hands around.

"She's my second," Franka added. Her hand rubbed the spot on Yagel's ribs where it was thickening.

"Ah, yes," Dr. Bennecort said. "Evan. What was he—ten or so—when it started?"

"Yes. I thought, at her age, it was too early, there should be lots of time."

"You know it can happen at any point. I had a patient who was sixty . . ."

"Yes, you told me," Franka said impatiently, and stopped herself. She took a moment to calm down, and the doctor waited. He was good—patient, professional—and Franka hoped that he could help. She wanted to say, "I'm imagining the worst," and have him reply, "The worst won't happen." She knew better, but she was hoping to hear it nonetheless.

It had happened suddenly. Franka was bathing her daughter the week before, cooing at the smiling, prattling darling of her life. After the shock of watching Evan go, she knew she was a little possessive. Franka smoothed the washcloth over the toddler's skin, gently swirling water over the perfect limbs, the wrinkles at the joints, the plum calves and shoulders. Yagel's skin was smooth and soft as a bruised fruit—except there, where she suddenly felt the thickness even through the washcloth.

She automatically talked back as Yagel babbled, but she felt her face freeze and Yagel noticed the difference in her touch and grew concerned, her legs pumping impatiently.

And Franka couldn't keep her hands off the child, touching, touching the spots that were changing, until Yagel began to get sore, and Simyon told her to go to the doctor. He said it coldly. He felt the spots that Franka felt, and he holed himself up deep inside, leaving Franka to find out the truth alone.

"She's my second," Franka whispered to the doctor. He'd been highly recommended by Deirdre, who had three emerald beetles tethered to her house, buzzing and smacking the picture window when the family sat down to watch TV. "We know their favourite shows," Dierdre said. "We know when they're happy."

Franka didn't want Yagel to end up like that, a child-sized insect swooping to her and away, eating from her palm. She wanted Yagel to end up a little girl.

"Time will tell," Dr. Bennecort said. Time. And blood

tests. Yagel screamed when the needle went in, but she forgot it all when given a lollipop. Maybe everything was still all right.

A month to get the results. And packets of information, numbers of people to talk to, a video explaining the process. He forgot she already had all this, from when Evan changed.

She didn't look at any of it, and neither did Simyon.

"I don't want this to happen," Franka whispered to her daughter, day and night. Yagel smiled back uncertainly.

"Don't you think you could love her, no matter what?" Deirdre asked cruelly when she came to lend her support. She so seldom left her home; she preferred to stay close to her emerald boys. Some people let their children go when they changed, gave in and released them. Took the ones that swam to the sea, and the ones that flew to the hills. The lucky ones kept the cats and dogs as pets—not *such* a change, after all—and put the ponies in the yard. You could wish for the higher orders; you could wish for the softer, cuddlier evolutions, but you couldn't change what was meant to be.

"But whatever they are, you love them, still," Deirdre said.

The three emerald beetles were about the size of a five-year-old child. They lifted and fluttered up and hit the window sometimes three at a time, with whirring thuds, they pulled to the ends of their cords, their green wings pulsing.

"My dears, my sweets," Deirdre thought as she stood on the inside of the picture window, her fingertips touching the glass as they swooped towards her, their hard black eyes intent. "My all, my all, my all."

She put out bowls for them, rotted things mixed with honey and vitamins, her own recipe, and rolled down the awning in case it rained, and went to Franka's house when she called, where she found her friend with her child in her arms.

"Feel this," Franka said. She rubbed a spot along Yagel's ribs. "It's thicker, isn't it? Not like the rest of her skin."

Deirdre took her fingers and delicately felt the spot. It felt like a piece of tape under the skin—less resilient, forming a kind of half-moon. "Yes," Deirdre said. "Maybe. It could be anything."

"Evan was ten," Franka whispered. "And she's only two. Your boys—did it happen at the same age for each?"

Deirdre shook her head. "Every one was different," she said, trying to find the right thing to say. "They're always different."

Every day, Yagel's skin thickened, making her arms and legs appear shorter. She no longer tried to stand up: crawling seemed to be more efficient. The first thick spot on her back now had a scale-like or plate-like appearance. Franka went to the library and began to look through books for an animal that matched: armadillo, no; rhino, no. And not elephant skin either. She skipped over whole sections, refusing to look at tortoises, lizards, snakes.

They were taught evolution as children, of course— the intimate, intricate link of the stages of life. Amoeba, fish, crawling fish, reptile; pupa, insect; egg, bird; chimp, ape, human; all the wonderful trigonometry of form and function. The beauty of it was startling. However life started, it changed. You were a baby once, then you're different. Each egg had its own revolution; no one stopped.

How beautiful it was to watch as characteristics became form, as the infant who loved water became a porpoise; as the toddler with the steady gaze became an owl, as the child who ran became a horse. It was magnificent. Her own brother had soared into the sky finally, a billowing crow (always attracted to sparkle, rakishly rowdy). She had envied him—his completion. She had stayed the same and felt a little cheated.

Still. Maybe it was less than magnificent when it was your own child. Or maybe her own reluctance was abnormal. Simyon told her gruffly, "Babies grow up, Franka. You know they change. You don't decide when it's time for them to go; *they* do. When it's right for them. Not for you."

He was not a sympathetic man—but had that always been true? No. He used to be interested in her worries; he used to want to soothe her rather than lecture. Although—she told herself—he was dealing with it, too. Both children evolving; leaving. So quickly gone. Of course it was hard for him, too.

She remembered her own brother's metamorphosis as a magical time—she had leapt up out of bed each morning to see the change in him overnight: a pouty mouth to a beak; dark fuzz on his shoulders into feathers; the way his feet cramped into claws; the tilt of his head and the glitter of his eye. It had been wonderful to see him fly, leaning out the window one minute, through it the next.

Even in the memory of it she heard her mother's

faltering cry. How stodgy her mother had seemed.

She leaned over Yagel. "I will always love you," she confided to the child's tender ear. Yagel poked her tongue out, clamped her arms to her side. "Always," Franka repeated. "Always."

Her neighbour Phoebe had two girls, neither of them evolved. She looked pregnant again and Franka went over to talk to her. "I think Yagel is evolving," she said. "You're so lucky." Of course it was wrong not to accept her children as they were, but she felt it in her, a deep reluctance to let go.

Phoebe nodded. "It's so nice to have them at home for so long, yes. Of course there's so much beauty in the changes—you know Hildy's girl?" Franka nodded. "A lunar moth. Elegant, curved wings. Extraordinary. Trembling on the roof. Hildy's taken photos and made an incredible silkscreen image. It's haunting. I look at some of the changes and it feels almost religious."

Phoebe's face looked dutiful and Franka knew a lie when she heard one: the false sincerity, the false envy. It was always better to have children who stayed children. And when they changed, there was always a judgement. No one really said it, but it was there. The mothers of sharks would always weep.

"You're too possessive," Simyon said, hunched over his dinner. He was eating quickly, tearing at his food. "Life is change." He finished his meal and prowled down the hall, going into his daughter's room, sniffing and blinking. "Reptile," he said, coming back. "Cold blood." He went off to watch his TV.

She drove around the next day, slowly. There were cages everywhere, some of them immense and gothic.

There were new ponds, and short bursts of trees. A huge, exquisite ceramic beehive stood next to a garage. She heard the trumpet of an elephant down the next road, and the scream of a peacock.

As she drove, heads poked from the corners of garages and from behind gazebos, some of them not yet completely determined.

Sometimes the changes were slow, and sometimes the changes were fast. Yagel stood up again and walked like a little girl—stubby, but a little girl. She prayed every day that her daughter would stay just as she was, prattling and dancing and observing the world. She'd give anything for that.

It was Deirdre who saw the change, coming one morning to visit Franka, hoping to convince her friend that all would be well. It was a sunny day and her boys were resting on rocks, showcasing the various shades of green and blue on their backs. She had watched them for an hour, admiring them, seeing how they were perfectly happy as they were. It gave her a terrific sense of peace, seeing that.

She brought photos along to show Franka—hoping she could point out the expressions in the boys' faces, proving they had full, rich lives so Franka could learn to let go. She hoped to persuade Franka that it wasn't the end; it was the beginning.

She knocked lightly and swung the back door open then paused when she heard an animal sound from inside. Rather close. She stood still, her hand on the handle of the open door. She could see the kitchen and part of the hallway, and hear a snorting, slobbering sound.

She wanted to close the door without making a sound, any sound, but as she stepped backwards her foot kicked a pail on the floor and she made a sound. It was just a small sound, a stupid sound. The animal noise inside stilled for a moment. The hairs on her arm prickled.

She heard sharp claws clicking on the floor, and she stepped back quickly, slamming the door. She saw the shadow crossing from the hallway and before she turned and ran, she looked.

It was Simyon, half-gone, spotted and hulking, his shoulders raised high, his hips trimmed of fat. His high hyena jaws were fresh with blood. Deirdre thought, for one quick moment, how mistaken poor Franka had been, how fatally misguided. She closed her eyes briefly. Whose blood was on Simyon's jaw: Franka's or Yagel's? Poor Franka, who had been blind to this evolution, delaying too long, thinking she was watching change while change crept up behind her. Deirdre headed home quickly, reminding herself it was Wednesday, the night of her sons' favourite show. She would pick up some fruit on the way home, at that store clear across town. Simyon wouldn't go in that direction and even if he did, he wouldn't be hungry for now.

THICK WATER

The sunset was orange again, strange, beautiful, and serene. It had a saffron edge, then it blended down to yellows, getting milder and milder the farther it spread along the horizon. It hung there slowly, spilling its colours gently across the sky, with a thin dash of red or rose blending then fading.

The ocean was almond-coloured, and slow. The biggest problem, Jenks said, was that she couldn't swim in it.

"Like swimming in a pillow," Brute snorted. "No, the biggest problem is we can't drink it. Tired of water rations. I mean, I'm okay with water rations unless I have to look at a whole lot of water all day."

"See, the real problem is, you insist on calling it water. If you stopped calling it water, you'd feel right as rain." This came from Squirrel, who always thought he had the essential point.

"Rain," Brute sighed, and they all stared out at the ocean, observing it. Was it water? It spread out wide against the horizon, as oceans did. But the water was thick and rolled; it was theoretically possible to walk on it, if you shifted your weight in the pockets the water formed and if you didn't go too quickly, which would cause a widespread line of waves, or worse, one of those sinkholes that never even glugged before it covered over.

They hadn't touched it; they still wore suits. But they had a piece of it in a tube in the lab room, and Sibbets was writing lots of meticulous things about it in her reports. Good for Sibbets. Brute didn't think they needed the suits any more; the air could be handled with just one of the simpler filters, a light mask over the nose and mouth. But Sibbets was cautious; Sibbets said wait.

The trolley wasn't due back for another year. The crew—two men, three women—had a habit of nicknaming everything, and the trolley was their name for the long-range transport.

Jenks, who was head of the exploratory team, said, "Maybe we're in at the beginning—you know, before life evolves."

"There's some kind of seaweed on the rocks," Darcy pointed out. He was polite and gorgeous and well bred, and Jenks—the reader in the group—had named him Darcy.

Their colony of two and a half domes was on the first shelf of a kind of stepped ascent from the beach. Discarded containers and broken equipment were left in the open next to it. There was no wind so they weren't careful about securing it.

They spent half the day outside, just poking around and observing, except for Sibbets who worked on her own inside. One day they gave themselves the task of examining the smooth, cigar-shaped stones that sat around on the lip of the beach.

It was natural, after handling the stones, to want to

wash the dust off their gloves. They went to the sea and cupped their hands and pulled out gobs of thick water. It amused them to carry the water around, and eventually they took some of it back to their collection of rocks. Darcy leaned over too far with his hands full, and he made it into a fake fall and rolled onto his back.

"Now look at that sunset," he said, pointing. His hand, blunted in its dirty tan glove, rose to the horizon.

The sunset was a long line of shadow, a pale hue up in the sky that drove along the surface in a line. It started from one direction and then—unlike an earthly sunset, which went down—it shifted around in a 180-degree arc. The light reflected off a series of moons, so it was handed across the horizon from left to right. It took hours. The sunrises were quieter, like pale ribbons. Midday was cream-coloured, with hints of salmon along the edges.

"Go get Sibbets," Jenks said. Squirrel ran inside, but Sibbets wouldn't come out.

"She said she can see it from inside," Squirrel reported.

Strike one against Sibbets, Jenks thought.

The rocks seemed smooth, but they must have had an abrasive component to them. Darcy found, one night, a tear in two places on his right glove. He got alcohol and cleaned his hands. Of course, he should report it. He didn't.

Jenks found a tear in her suit, around her knee. She put it in the daily report. They were out of range, now; there was no one to check with, to discuss it with. She didn't want to alarm her junior officers.

Darcy got a new glove and saw within a day that it had shredded along the wrist. Nothing had happened to him after the first hole, so when Brute said, "Damn, my suit's ripped!" Darcy said, "It doesn't matter. Mine ripped a week ago. I'm fine."

They were coming inside. Jenks heard them both. She didn't say anything; she kept thinking about it at dinner. "My suit was torn too," she said finally. "No signs of anything."

"You can't be sure," Sibbets said. "An alien bacteria, a disease—who says you would know by now? Take some antibiotics, get some new suits."

"We're pretty much already done for, if we're done for," Darcy said.

Sibbets, always in her lab, could be seen as a figure bending over or lifting things, tapping at her computer or putting something in a jar. They could see her through the plexi-window; she never seemed to look for them.

"She's so stuck," Darcy said. "Never tries anything. Never takes a risk. And she calls herself an explorer."

"She calls herself a scientist," Brute said.

"*I'm* the explorer," Squirrel said. The face window on his suit showed a big grin. He lifted his hands and took off the hood.

"Put that back on," Jenks said.

"Look at my hands." Squirrel lifted them up and showed the holes. "The air's been getting in for two weeks, at least. Let me tell you," he said, breathing in deep, his nostrils working, "it's got a strange smell." He sucked in air so hard his chest rose up. "Spicy." His chest relaxed. "Good."

"Oh hell," Brute said, taking off her hood as well. "It's not like I haven't done it already. I've been out sniffing it when no one's looking. I swear, sir, it's harmless." She looked at Jenks and saluted.

Darcy already had his off. "Sir," he said, "the smell gets better at sunset. It has something to do with the colours, I think."

They looked at Jenks, waiting. She considered the facts: they were all exposed anyway. So she took her hood off. The air was moist, which was surprising; the sea never evaporated, it just rolled around. There was never moisture on their suits. But the smell was good, indeed.

"The colours are brighter," Brute said, looking at the sea. Even though it wasn't evening yet, the colours wove into the sky: yellow, saffron, salmon, butter, carnelian, ruby, blood.

They shed their hoods and then they shed their suits. The weather was perfect. There seemed no variation in temperature as they felt it. They did keep on shoes, because the arches of their feet were always tender, but they stripped down to their underwear.

And then they began touching the water.

It was irresistible. "Did you notice the variations?" Brute asked. "The variations of shade. How it runs from almond to cream? How you can watch the colours move?"

"To think I didn't notice it before," Darcy said. "What do you think caused that? The hoods? Maybe it was too subtle to make it through that plastic window of ours."

"Plastic window," Jenks laughed. "I think so. Look at Sibbets, now, she doesn't notice anything." They turned and looked at Sibbets, who straightened up and looked out at them, then turned away again.

"See that colour there," Squirrel said, pointing. "The

way it laps." They came up next to each other, forming a line. They stood very close. They were naked along their arms and legs, and they pulled in close to each other, so their skin touched. "I would hate to leave this place."

"True, it's getting to be more and more like home." This was from Brute, who stepped forward and bent down, scooping up a ball of water. "All the comforts." Her face got a sudden illumination and her eyes narrowed a little and she got a wicked grin. She looked at the ball of water in her hand, said, "Here goes, kids," and neatly split it in two, dropping half and popping the other half in her mouth.

Jenks wasn't fast enough to stop her, and it would have been half-hearted anyway. They understood each other better, so they all knew that they agreed with Brute: test the water. The air had proved to be all right, the temperature was perfect. They had never felt better, never been happier. Sibbets in her little window looked ridiculous; out here, in the creamy sunlight, near the iridescent sea—out here was a higher order of perfection.

Still, they watched as Brute swallowed and her eyes went internal, tracking the feel of the water going down.

"Brute? What's it like?" Jenks took a step closer.

Brute sighed. "It's good." She looked around, to the sea, the horizon, the rock shelf behind them. "It's very satisfying. I can feel it."

Brute was fine that day and the next and the next. Jenks caught Darcy and Squirrel pulling small rolls of water from the edge, pushing it around in their palms, eating it. She watched in silence.

"Everything's sharper," they said. "Not at the edges, no, in the centre. It's hard to describe, but it's great. Don't be afraid."

That was from Darcy, who whispered to her. Jenks was already considering it. She bent down and pulled a bead of water out. It had soft edges, reforming slowly. She took it in her mouth, rolled it on her tongue, and swallowed.

"Well," Darcy said. "Welcome to the club."

The thick water was all they needed—that and the gray seaweed that formed like a frost along certain rocks; slightly crisp, a small taste that lingered. "You guys are nuts," Sibbets said tightly when they showed dutifully up for meals. "You don't know what's going to happen, the effects, the long-term significance. You've left me all alone here now. If something happens, I'm the only one who can take care of you."

"You could join us," Brute said, shrugging. "We're not so bad. And you'll have more fun."

"I have work to do," Sibbets answered, lowering her eyes. She ate her food industriously, chewing vigorously and swallowing carefully. They all watched her.

"Why are you watching me?" she said finally.

"You don't look comfortable with us," Squirrel said.

Sibbets put down her fork. "You're not wearing clothes. You don't eat. You stare at me when you come in. You eat the water. None of you is acting normal." She looked around the room. They looked at her, all of them, and they were all smiling. One by one, they held their hands out to her. "You should come with us," one of them said. She couldn't tell which one.

The next day Brute came up to the plexi-window. Sibbets didn't see her at first; she was waiting for the centrifuge to stop spinning. She had no hope that anything new would be discovered, but she was thorough. If she did a test once, she did a test twice.

She looked up to relieve her eyes from the fine work. She looked out the plexi-window.

And there was Brute, grinning at her through the window, staring and grinning, her lips pulling back more and more from her teeth. Brute's eyelids rose even higher and she moved back as if confounded, then she pushed her head fast against the window. Sibbets could even see the plexi move a little, and she was annoyed.

What if she broke it? Sibbets stood up, raised her hand, about to yell, when her hand dropped and her mouth opened.

Brute's face was smack against the plexi-window, yes, and it was entirely flat. Like a balloon against the plexi. Sibbets stared, her mind slowing down, trying to make it into some trick, when Brute slowly peeled her flat face off the window, and Sibbets watched as the face reshaped itself, back to Brute's face. Even then, she stood frozen, waiting for some explanation to occur to her, something sensible. Brute stared at her, winked at her!

Sibbets stood there, trying to think, watching Brute wave at the others, who were standing together and watching. They all met together, waving arms gently, bobbing in and out. She could almost feel how much they gravitated together. In the old days, they wouldn't have tolerated that. Everyone had been conscious of personal space.

She spent the afternoon wondering if she had caught some kind of dementia; if she were seeing things. She checked herself and doubted herself and shivered a little, and took some antibiotics.

They ate less and less, yet they seemed healthy. They came to dinner most of the time, arriving together and staying for a while, then drifting away. Drifting. Well, it was hardly drifting with all that laughter. They giggled together, they cast glances together, they squealed with joy when Sibbets asked if they had done their reports, if they had checked any of the equipment, if they had brought more samples.

"Samples?" Darcy asked. "Samples?" And with that he pulled a hair out of his head. He held it out dramatically and then dropped it into the soup. His cohorts laughed again. Sibbets could feel herself tense: laughter laughter laughter. They were monsters.

"I don't like that," she said. "That's food. Who knows what contamination—"

"Absolutely none," Jenks said. "You can write that down somewhere."

Sibbets looked at the captain cautiously. She had gotten thinner, tauter, quicker, but there was a little blurring around the edges. Her chin wasn't exactly the same shape. Could that be possible?

The rest of them all looked at Sibbets eagerly, as if she might perform. Then they laughed again, their bodies bouncing around. They each rested their right hand on their stomachs, as if the laughing hurt.

Sibbets lowered her head and ate her soup. When she was finished, she looked around. None of them had eaten and they were all still looking at her, expectantly.

"What?" she said.

"We can see that soup move down your esophagus," Squirrel said. "Like going down a drain."

"No you can't," Sibbets said.

"We have x-ray vision," Brute said. And she winked.

Sibbets's heart was racing. "If you guys don't eat, then I'm going to stop cooking for you. We shouldn't waste food. But you have to eat?" She had changed her tone halfway through, careful not to be out of line. The captain was her superior, after all.

"We eat the *urden*," Jenks said.

"Urden?"

"The seaweed thing. It's delicious. And it takes care of your appetite for hours, maybe days. You don't need much and your whole body feels light and clear."

"You shouldn't eat it!" Sibbets burst out. "How do you know what it will do to you?"

"We *do* know what it will do to us," Brute said, standing up. "*Because* we've eaten it."

And they stood up smoothly, all together, and faced her. All their faces looked the same, and Sibbets couldn't be sure if she was looking at Brute or Jenks or Darcy or Squirrel. How could all their faces look the same? She wanted to weep, but she never did that. It was just this sense of total frustration, this sense that it had gotten away from her. Could this be some kind of hallucination?

"I think I'm sick," she said finally. "I keep seeing things that can't be."

"Oh really," the person most on her left said. "Like what?"

"You keep changing. Physically." She lifted her head. "Right now, I can't tell any of you apart."

"You're all cooped up," Brute said (if it was Brute). "That's the problem."

"Come out and play!" Squirrel hooted.

"I'm a scientist," Sibbets said feebly. "I don't think

what you're doing is right. It's untested. We don't know what will happen."

"It's funny. You said 'we.' *We're* the we, now. You're just an I."

Who said that, Sibbets wondered, squinting a little. Was it Darcy? Or Squirrel?

"Awfully lonely," Jenks said. "Isn't it?"

And with that, they left, like a bunch of puppets. Thank God they slept outside. She cleaned up, wiping down the chairs and the table with antibacterials. They were "off," she was sure of it. They had abandoned their duties, such as they were. They had, really, abandoned her. And she thought, again and again, this is unforgiveable. It gave her a small sense of triumph, that she could define their behaviour that way. But the sense of anger faded—what good did it do, after all, to blame them for their actions? They had bonded. They had excluded her. Against all the rules. Against advice. How could they do it, do something so fundamentally wrong? Her anger was rising again. Leaving her to face it all alone!

She felt it strongly. She was the one now who had to maintain civilization on this planet. Was that it—had they gone native? What could that mean in a place with no natives? She stared out the plexi-window, scanning the beach for them. There they were now, knee deep in that thick water. One of them bent down, snaking her arm into the water. From this distance, it looked like the arm became part of the water.

She turned her back on them. It was up to her to do all the work, then. She went back to her office. She would stop preparing food for them. Until they changed their behaviour, it was nothing more than an ordeal for her, and a farce if they didn't eat. It would keep them from slipping something in the food, too; that had to be a consideration. If they could drop a contaminated hair in, who knew what else. . . . What if they snuck some of that water in, behind her back?

She would lock them out during mealtimes because, really, they were no longer members of her team. That was true, wasn't it? She stopped and looked out the window. They weren't there, so she moved into the next dome and looked through that window.

There they were, she realized with a jolt, standing lined up, all facing her. Just standing. And then they all waved at her and walked away.

A feeling of exhaustion overcame her, and a longing for someone to talk to about it. Then she saw them walking into the water, sinking down, and disappearing. No bubbles, no outstretched hand (just as well: what would she do in that case?).

And then they slowly rose again. It was very graceful, but she found herself straining for air long before she could see the tops of their heads slowly begin to surface.

It did look beautiful. They did look happy. She wasn't happy, that much was certain. But she had no inclination to join them, whatever they were doing. If, in some future time, they proved themselves to be right, proved her to be wrong—fine.

The next day, she didn't open the door to let them in for meals. She could hear their voices, now, very dimly, all of them sounding exactly the same. Sometimes they were right outside her window, saying things, as if speaking to her. But the words sounded made-up. She wouldn't put that past them, that they were speaking some language not their own. Or, well, not hers. Too infuriating, really. Like pig-Latin, meant to point out how she didn't fit in.

Each morning she got up and wrote her report and transmitted it although it went nowhere—the planets blocked her words from reaching anyone. It was comforting all the same. In less than a year, some morning not unlike this one, she would hear a blip, a beep, some startled movement on the line. It would be a warm voice, a human voice, a relief after all this weirdness—and maybe this wasn't even the end of it, maybe they would become sand or rock or pellets of water themselves (she couldn't know)—there would be a voice over the line, telling her, You made it. You were right to seal that door. You are the one who is valuable. You are the one who saved the mission, and we adore you.

And she liked the sound of that so much—the love that was in that voice—that she began to fear that Jenks or Brute or Squirrel or Darcy would knock on the door someday and ask to come in. And she would be uncertain. She would want to open the door because for once they would sound normal. And they would complain they were hungry. How would she be able to withstand that? If they did that? Or if they bumped their foreheads against the plexi-window, crying, "Sibbets, Sibbets, we're sorry, let us in!"

That would be unfair. To endure for almost all the way, and then have them trick her like that at the end. She would have to set up some rules. She would be clear about what they could and could not do. If they wanted food, she would leave it outside. That was reasonable. If they wanted anything else, they could leave her a note.

She found a notebook and pen to give them and suited up. Just because they had survived without a suit didn't mean she would change procedure. Who knew what was growing inside their brains or in their blood vessels, biding its time?

She waited for the air lock to empty, then she stepped outside. Where were they now? They'd been in sight before she suited up. She turned around and bam! Something hit her. She dropped the notebook, staggering a little. She still held on to the pen.

Then another strike. Her mind was trying to figure it out. She looked down at her arm and saw something moving down it. Like oil.

It was the thick water, of course. She turned to the left, and another one hit her.

"Can Sibbets come out and play?" Squirrel called, his voice high and squeaky. He had his own face today, Sibbets saw.

"Stop it," Sibbets said. "It isn't funny."

Someone put a hand on her, from behind. She twisted as best she could in the suit. It was Jenks. "We miss you, Sibbets. It's hard to command someone who stays inside all day. Don't you feel like you're in prison?"

"I'm not sure who's in prison," Sibbets answered. "I'm happier inside."

"But I want you out here," Jenks said. "I order you."

"Yes, sir," Sibbets said, backing up. "Just let me stow my gear and I'll be right back."

Someone laughed. "Fat chance." That was Brute. "Just get her helmet off."

She was close to the door, close enough to get in and slam it.

That was that, then. Her heart was pounding. She went to the clean room. She stood under the spray. When she was done, she took off her suit. One of the clasps for the helmet had been undone. Luckily, they hadn't gotten further than that.

There really was no reason to go outside anymore. But they knew everything about the domes—could she really keep them from coming in?

If she wanted to survive, she would have to get rid of them. Her hands got very still; she clasped them together in her lap. The idea was horrific. Could she really kill them? No, it was too much. She could never be driven that far. If she stayed inside, and they stayed outside, then there was no reason for it. They would just keep to their own sides of the door.

Late one night, just as she was drifting off, she heard a scratching sound. Something small and rough. Was she imagining it? She took a flashlight and inched her way towards the sound. It was coming from the next dome, but it stopped as she neared it. Of course: she had passed a plexi-window; they had seen the light.

They moved around like mice, nibbling here and there; were they using their fingernails? Did they still have fingernails? They could be using the rocks to scrape away at the dome, making the walls here and there thinner and thinner, so that one night they might poke their hands through and pull her out.

Maybe she couldn't just sit and wait for rescue; that was too far off. What were they thinking about? What were they planning?

She was a scientist; she could fight them. She thought about how to kill them, now. She reminded herself that they were aliens, they were after her. Sometimes they stood, one at each plexi-window, just to frighten her, to say she couldn't escape them. Well, she could. She could escape them if they were dead.

She hated having to think this way—and who was responsible for *that*? Who was forcing her to think of *that*?

It would have to be something that got them all together, all at once. That meant an explosion. Yes, blow them up entirely, leave no trace. They were fond of standing together like forks. Good.

There was a set of explosives and a remote fuse, two in fact. She took them to the kitchen table and read the instructions. It was easy. She took off the wrappings and stopped.

She sat at the table, her hands shaking.

She began to keep records about their movements. When she rose, she checked all the windows, recording where they were. They were almost always together. Sometimes one or two broke off and went up the rocky inclines. Did they still eliminate, then, and have the need for privacy? Were they mating?

She heard scraping again. In the daytime. So now she had two reasons to go out: to see if they really were trying to scratch through the walls, and to set up the explosives, just in case. She didn't have to use them; it was merely a precaution.

So. Where should she place the explosives? She went back to her log. They liked to appear in her windows, but usually one by one for that. They liked to go as a group to the thick water, but that was too far away, and the water would probably shield them. Occasionally they picked through the rubble of the trash heap and took a scrap of something.

She decided to take out some small objects, to put them along with the explosives, in the trash heap. She decided on a toothbrush, a cup, a candy bar. The candy bar would make it seem like she was trying to see if they still ate; that would satisfy their curiosity.

She watched from the plexi-window. The first day they didn't go in the water; they merely stood about. The second day only two of them went in. The scratchings continued overnight, like animals pawing at the door to get in. On the third day, she was rewarded.

They all went in the thick water, sliding through it and then sliding down, until their feet vanished, their hips vanished, their heads vanished. Sibbets suited up, unbolted the door and walked out. She walked around the domes. Yes, there were scratches; there were areas that had been peeled away. She thought maybe it had proved too hard for them, until she circled around to the back, where her lab was. There was a bigger spot here, a more delicate spot. She tapped her foot against it, and it gave slightly. Her heart pounded. They were distracting her, she thought, with scratching at other places so she wouldn't concentrate on this spot.

Her mouth was dry. She looked at the beach and saw that someone's head was showing through the line of the water. She moved quickly to the trash heap and put out the items, hiding the explosives under a bit of trash. She saw that three of them were kicking their way out of the water, pushing themselves to shore. She waved (sarcastically), and went inside.

Let them think what they would.

There was no doubt in her mind that they were about to break in. She went to the lab room, got down on her knees, pressing against the wall until she found the soft spot. It wouldn't take them long. She placed a plastic sheet over it and taped around it. This would protect her against a breach, temporarily at least.

If they stopped scratching at the walls, she would leave them alone. She would give them that chance, one last chance. It was not her decision; it was theirs.

She folded herself into her bed that night, hoping there would be nothing but silence around her. But the scratching started, the little nibblings at the wall; that night, they seemed to be at all the walls from all sides. Had she missed other spots that were just as well worn as the one in the lab?

She bolted upright. She turned the lights on, crouching and running through the domes, listening. The sounds stopped as she drew near, then they started up somewhere else, as if they were tracking her, aware of her every move.

She ran around, and wherever she thought a sound had come from, she pounded her fist just above it (she would not push her hand through a weakened spot, no, she wouldn't be pushed to that kind of error); to the top at first and then over to the right or to the left, she varied it because she didn't want them to work out how she would act.

She did it for hours, skittering around, hating them, for the sounds, for their concentration, for their harmony—they were working in concert against her; if one of them weakened, there was another and she only had her wits and her sense and her logic and her hard, hard determination.

In the afternoon, she blew them up. They finally came to see what she had laid out in the trash heap, picking up the toothbrush, holding up the cup. They came as they usually did, and she pulled the switch and there was a muffled boom! And they were shattered, just like that.

She didn't have the nerve to go out and look, not right away. She waited until she stopped shaking, and then she wrote down, again, her reasons: How they didn't eat, how they drank the water. The way they were breaking in. That they wanted to infect her.

She added to her notes: they would bring the pollution back to Earth.

She stayed inside for two days. She was used to being inside, but there was something in her heart, in her mind, somewhere, that wanted her to go outside. To see. Just to check. Something.

Finally she suited up, quite slowly, took the laser guns, and let herself out. She turned around carefully, surveying the area before moving to the blast site. The hole the explosion had made was deeper than she'd thought it would be. There was a glittering along the walls. Metallic ash? She surveyed it warily, some ten yards away. Most of the debris would be plastics, with some metal. There shouldn't be much dust. She moved closer, squinting through the window of her helmet. She was afraid there would be blood, but she couldn't see any blood.

She spun around. For a moment she'd felt that someone was watching her. But there was no one. Of course there was no one.

She was close now, standing at the edge of the blackest part, just looking slowly around, along the ground, checking the bits and pieces of things. She glanced quickly, not knowing what there was she could be afraid of.

A movement. She scanned along the outside wall of the dome. Something, yes, something small. A piece that had stuck to the wall was now, slowly, falling down.

And another. Yes, very small. That's why it was so hard to see, there were drops of things moving down the wall. Her heart lurched but she thought she had to verify it, she would imagine things if she didn't.

She walked up to the wall and bent over slightly, peering at it.

A piece of flesh down at the bottom of the wall, on the ground. How had it survived? She stared at it. Something else slid down the wall. So small, like a drop, and while she watched it fell at the edge of the skin and joined it.

She straightened up suddenly. That glittering—the wall seemed to have a sheen; it wavered a little. She told herself to stop thinking, to stop anticipating. She forced her body to still itself, she made herself stare, unblinking, at the steady, slow accretion of the sheen, so that the thin wet slick of it gathered, getting thicker, until it pooled to a heavy drop. There were drops here and there, small ones that gathered weight from another small one nearby, others that never moved and seemed to be waiting.

Some of them shivered, impatiently. They hovered against the wall until the weight shifted them down to a drop below them, or slightly to the side.

As she watched, she could see the largest one fall down minutely, shifting to the left, heading for the skin on the ground. Then it joined it. Of course it was still small, it was skin, yes, but just a bit of skin.

Sibbets leaned over it. She bent closer. Another drop found it and it moved, just a little. The tip of a finger. She waited again, without moving, until the silvery, sheeny stuff—thick water, she knew it—formed another drop, and reached it. She could see where the top sliver of the fingernail was just starting to be visible. It was being built in front of her.

Sibbets sucked in the air inside her helmet. Was there no relief from this kind of horror? They would assemble themselves every day, bit by bit, until she would wake one morning and find a balloon-face pressed against the plexi-window, or all four of them, touching at the shoulder, just standing together and pointing at her. It was unbearable—the thought that they would be there again, *knowing what she'd done*—she could feel her eyes rolling back in her head. She could hear herself whimper.

And the scratchings would begin again. Her shoulders tightened. She would be inside, listening to them claw their way to her, grinning, nodding, blending, aiming themselves at her. She could see, indeed, that they had turned into a joint organism; organism, yes, not people, and she should dispel any lingering trace of regret or guilt.

She went back to her lab for comfort. She stood and looked around, at the shelves of specimens—mostly the thick water. There were plastic jars and glass jars. They were all sizes, and there was a whole container of more jars in the clean room.

She thought her way through it, and then she assembled her materials the next day—jars, lids, pipettes, scoops, tweezers—and put on her suit. She carried the things carefully to the ruined dome. The wall still glistened faintly, but on the ground there were small staggered movements as globules combined. She took her first plastic cup and ticked her eyes along the ground, evaluating. That finger she had seen the day before was now assembled to the tip of the cuticle. But there was a piece of the top of the head complete with hair, far to the right. Next to that a bone with a scrap of sinew. A piece of beige skin inched towards it. She began to index, in her head, any recognizable thing. An elbow, a rib, a foot nearly complete and flexing hopefully. She bent over, watching. The things moved; they had purpose. "Probably dying to get together again," she thought, and smiled. She could stop that.

She opened jars and took the larger parts, and the moveable parts—she would have none of them wandering away, gathering behind a rock or in the sea, repairing.

Every other day she went out, gathering with her jars and vats, picking out the hearts, the tongues, the scar on Jenks' thigh, two tattoos (was that Squirrel or Darcy?).

The hearts and lungs and guts could wait; they were going nowhere. Feet and hands had to come first, but the heads—no, they would be gathered in pieces. It was too disturbing, even for her analytic bent, her Euclidean eye. It was enough that she would reassemble them in her mind, put the puzzle together, intellectually. Let it remain intellectual—let her surmise that the jar on the top shelf belonged with the jar on the bottom shelf, cheek-by-jowl, brow to chin. They were like lovers who were no good for each other and should be kept apart.

Or, at least, no good for her.

She gathered them, plucking them and sorting them.

Would they only truly recognize their own or would they pollinate—making a Brute-Darcy, a Squirrel-Jenks, a Squirrel-Darcy? They had ballooned into each other; they might have the desire to form one interconnected being: eight legs, eight arms, four hearts, one mind.

One brain bloomed and she bottled it, not waiting for the brainpan to find its home. Four brains, each on a shelf. They might have achieved telepathy; she would see.

So, at the end, over the course of two weeks, she spooned them up, in segments or in parts, and jarred them. At first she kept them dry, then she thought—mercifully thought, scientifically thought; or heroically thought: they want the water.

She went down to the sea, and carved out a piece in her bucket, and brought it back, weighted with virtue. And she cut off pieces into each jar, tightening the lids—no hokum from them, delighting in the water—and sealed them tight.

In six months, in five months, in four months, in three—soon, soon, there would be a beep on her screen, the first text from home.

"How are you?" it would ask, and she would sit down, a smile on her face, her hands slightly shaking. The eyes behind her, blinking, the hearts beating, the lungs insisting on their own thick-water breathing—all of them watching, and she would type:

We are well.

THE HAIR

Truly the most astonishing thing happened when that new employee Mindy walked into the meeting wearing Paulina's hair.

Paulina's hands immediately went up to her head. Bald. Maybe a little patch of stubble.

Paulina gasped, but her coworkers at the meeting smiled a bland welcome to Mindy. Couldn't they see what had happened?

Paulina's hands began to shake in anger. Her pencils had been disappearing, even her scotch tape. And now this!

She knew perfectly well that women without hair didn't last long, speaking corporately. Management was hairist. Paulina had always maintained a middle-of-the-road hairdo: pretty much all one length to her earlobes, parted on the right side, with the back sort of wedge-cut. Mindy hadn't bothered to change the part, even, and the colour and length of the bangs were exactly the same. "Good haircut, Mindy," Ron Unterling said in his loud I'm-top-dog tones. Mindy beamed, but the edge of her eyes wickedly slid Paulina's way.

"Well, well, well," Ron said. "Enough about hair."

So the meeting on the Reports went on as if nothing unusual had happened. Reports celebrated the status quo, and Paulina was a big proponent of the status quo, since it paid her a pretty good salary for very little effort. Her job consisted of making up questions and answers used to evaluate and categorize various corporate projects. She looked at what the company was doing and found a way of discussing it so that it seemed innovative and generous. She liked to look on the positive side of life, generally, and that had seemed to work so far.

But she was beginning to think things had changed, as Ron beamed upon the company. "The Report on Reports is coming up, and I thought this year we'd push our presentations to the limit. You know, liven it up, throw in a joke. Put some zip in their zippers. We're going to make this the best review ever!" He looked around at the fawning faces. "See what you can do. Put extreme into the routines! How's the Facilitation Report, Paulina?"

"As you can see by looking at—let me see—page 2," she began, "the main delays in project completion or status achievement break down into: personnel indecision, end-usage misidentification . . ."

"It's a beautiful Report," Ron interrupted. He had never interrupted her before. "And so long." His smile paused for a second, just enough for Paulina's heart to throw out a mismanaged beat.

"I try to be thorough," she said defensively (always a mistake: the zebra about to be corrected by the lion surely has just that tone).

Ron nodded and Paulina slumped slightly in relief. "All the information is here. It just needs a little jazzing up. I think Mindy could help you there. A little of her style added to your expertise would really sell it."

Mindy smiled gaily; Paulina tried to keep her eyes from darting around the room. "I didn't realize you wanted style," she said plaintively.

Ron looked over to Mindy and then back to her. "I do," he said.

Paulina had never asked a hard question because she had never wanted an unpleasant answer, but that was not the way Mindy worked at all. "Way too obvious," Mindy said, crossing out things on the printout Paulina handed her. "You're letting everyone off easy. Let's have some fun with this." She gave a little shake to her head; her hair shook with it.

"That's a beautiful hairstyle," Paulina said as nicely as she could. She wanted to see if Mindy would show any guilt at all.

"Why, uh, thank you." Mindy seemed to be searching for something to say in return. "I like yours, too. It must be so easy to take care of."

"I used to have hair like that," Paulina continued.

"I don't recall."

"Exactly like that."

"Well, I'm sure it will grow back." Mindy smiled and turned away.

But it didn't grow back. By the next week there was no more fuzz than there had been. She began to wear a hat. One day Mindy tapped her on the shoulder.

"Excuse me," Mindy said, "I don't mean to be rude or anything, but your hat is bothering people."

"Bothering people? How?"

"Well, they *stare* at it," Mindy said. "They're trying to figure it out. You know: *why* is she wearing a hat? Is she covering something up? Didn't you notice how many times Jim said 'cap' at this morning's meeting? It's very distracting."

"There was a meeting this morning? I wasn't even there."

"See? That's how bad it is." Mindy was quietly triumphant in a sympathetic kind of way. She had one of those deliberately soft voices that are supposed to be nonthreatening, legally.

And Mindy handed her a memo Ron had signed that specifically requested no hats unless for religious or medical reasons. "Well, I suppose that's not a *medicinal* hat?" she asked with raised eyebrows. "Although it looks like it might be. . . ."

One fundamental problem was that Mindy's mind was sharper than Paulina's. Sharp, Paulina thought, as in: sees things clearly; as in: cuts without conscience.

Mindy removed most of Paulina's questions and added this: Do you blame your boss for the delay or incompletion?

It was a jarring yes-no question and it was bound to get someone in trouble, maybe even cost some jobs. Mindy was revising the Report in such a way that it would be necessary to actually recommend some action. Paulina had expected to retire in thirty years or so, and she could only last thirty more years by keeping herself neutral and pleasant, but she was beginning to find her nerves snapping, her teeth grating, her head filling with explosive scenarios.

And there was something in the alert way everyone was looking lately that manifestly signalled the scent of blood. Change was coming, and change was not good.

Without hair, Paulina felt conspicuous. If people stared, she believed she looked monstrous. And if they didn't look she was left in doubt: was she now somehow unnoticeable? Had she been dismissed from the world? She was thrown off her track; she was losing her way.

The next week Paulina appeared in a wig that matched the hair she used to have. A few heads looked at her with interest. She saw Mindy glaring: the eyelids lowered; the upper lip raised. "What a nice haircut," Mindy said in her oh-so-nice voice. "It looks somehow familiar."

Paulina smiled at her vaguely. "Does it?" Someone down the table snickered.

Ron settled forward in his chair, his hands almost gripping the table. "We've got a new twist on the Reports this year; we've hired a Talent consultant for the presentations leading up to the Report on the Reports," he said. "I've got an emcee to introduce each presentation of each individual Report, and to break it up, a magician in the middle, with a disappearing tiger. This year we'll also have a choice of four entrées, all of them quite tasty. No mistakes like last year's incident of the live goat." He looked around benevolently. "We just need good, thorough Reports and a relaxed presentation. You can't have a top-tier company without creativity, and that's where we're going—creative! Top tier!"

He started around the table, reviewing the area of each Report and discussing who would present it. Paulina had represented her section the year before and expected to do it again. Ron got all the way around the table before reaching Mindy and Paulina. He beamed fondly at Mindy, who put her hand up to stroke her hair modestly. Paulina lifted her own hand automatically.

"Now, Mindy," Ron said, "tell us what you have in mind. You'll be in charge of the section on questionnaires and appraisals."

At that, Paulina's hand dropped slowly, chastened. Mindy was now above her! When had the re-org happened, or was it still secret?

First the hair, then her rank. Paulina felt that she was all alone on the savannah, with something hungry moving towards her. Ron had said to rev it up, and she would do that. And she would take him by surprise to boot.

She went to everyone she'd interviewed before, going backwards through the questionnaires. She'd always filed the responses anonymously, of course, except for the letter coding in the top right hand of the first page, which indicated which department was involved and the initials of the employee.

"Have I ever stolen anything is one of the questions now," Mort on the third floor said, holding the latest version of the questionnaire in his hand. "Have *they*? Don't they steal my spirit while paying for my mind? What kind of questions are these? Number 91 asks if I've ever had sex in the office. *That's* the only interesting question, and even that's none of their business. But I'd like to know about the others, of course, the ones without offices. Are they using mine? Sometimes my chairs have been moved."

"It's a trick question. If you're thinking about that, it shows you're not working," Paulina said. "It's diabolical, actually, since once we ask the question we force you to think about it. I know what questions can do to people. They're metaphysical, aren't they? I never realized it before, how much I like questions. They're the building blocks of reason!" She grinned somewhat foolishly, but she felt strangely moved. "I love my job," she said. "I never knew it before. I love making questions."

Mort looked at her sympathetically. "Just when they've started taking your questions away, too; that's what they call irony, isn't it?"

Paulina offered to present a small report on the residue of Reports; i.e., does anyone remember last year's Reports? It tickled Ron, since she could go through his predecessors' Reports and mock them.

"You can have ten minutes tops," he said, "or the sherbet will melt."

Paulina was guaranteed a position, which was now what mattered. She lied about how she was going to do the Report; she had something else up her sleeve. Always before, she had made up questions that everyone knew how to answer; what were the questions everyone knew how to ask?

In the meantime, she wore her wig slightly askew. It made Mindy self-conscious. Paulina began to dress better, too; she wouldn't go so far as to say she was mimicking Mindy; she was buying clothes that were like Mindy's, however, and she wore garments similar to Mindy's the day after her rival did. She was working up to wearing them the day before.

She asked Mort: "What are the questions that really matter to you?"

"My top ten are: Is there a terrible disease beginning in me, how long will I live, is my wife faithful, are my kids good, do people respect me, why am I not happier, where is the money I deserve? If that's not ten, it doesn't matter," he said.

Paulina wrote down them down and went to the departments and people she had interviewed before. "When will I be happy?" they asked, "And am I dying?"

They did their projects even in the middle of these questions. "Can my father hear me in his coma?" one asked. "How much pain can my daughter stand? Why am I afraid? Is there God, is there God, is there God?"

Paulina wrote the questions down frantically and began to organize them so they changed subtly but progressively from "When will I be happy?" to "Where is my true home in all this?" to "Why am I afraid?"

Through it all, of course, she wore her wig, unable to regain her hair by any natural means. Mindy certainly wouldn't be shamed into giving the hair back, so what was Paulina to do?

The Report on Reports loomed large, as did all the questions associated with it, which Paulina now considered in all their serious political consequences. Historically the Reports had been used to eliminate people, to repress people—certainly in that regard all the janitorial and support staff were consistently repressed by the sheer fact that no questionnaire was ever directed their way.

So she asked the building super and the janitors and cleaning women. She spoke to the secretaries and the temps and the phone-system administrators. Their questions were the same as Mort's, only with a few more about money. Paulina was excited by the pathos of their wonder, by the exactness of their needs.

"I don't agree with some of your questions," she told Mindy. Mindy, after all, was still doing Paulina's section of the Reports, gathering the responses to the latest questionnaire.

Mindy shrugged. "You don't have to," she said easily. "We're trying something different. You'll understand eventually." At that she grinned a full, white-tooth grin, the pose of a benevolent predator. Paulina could feel the lion's eye sweep towards her; she felt in danger of being culled. The herd never actually *sees* the one who gets eaten, she thought; they look away from the kill. She wanted to force them to look, all of them.

Paulina knew what she wanted to do. "We're going to sing our Report," she told Mort and Joe, a super, and Yvonne, a cleaning woman. "We're going to change their hearts with the power of our questions."

"There are some Voices on the staff," Yvonne agreed. "I hear them late at night, emptying the pails."

"Henry has a voice like a boom box," Joe added. "And the moves, he moves like a wave. He should be out in front."

"We will *all* be in front," Paulina declared, "in our own individual ways. We need to show how strong we are." Her wig felt like it was slipping; she righted it. Yvonne and Mort modestly averted their eyes, and it made Paulina waver. She might be endangering them. "On the other hand, it might be risky. Maybe we shouldn't do it," she said softly.

"I've never been in a Report," Yvonne said. "And I've been cleaning these offices for twenty years."

Joe nodded "We want to do it. This is our one chance."

The Reports took all afternoon. The minor Reports came first, like warm-up bands; they weren't expected to grab attention. Ron glowed with achievement; he was obviously being groomed for promotion and it looked like Mindy would replace Ron when he left. All Paulina's hopes of anonymous longevity were squashed.

Mindy wore an iridescent pearl-coloured body stocking with a long pearl-coloured skirt with tremendous slits. She threw out numbers as if she'd made them up. "Fine fractals advanced to 78 by knocking out the middle," she said and did a split, her arms thrown upwards. "Move the work downwards and pack them in together."

The crowd roared at Mindy's dance; the bosses nudged each other. Mindy humbly bowed with arms crossed over her breasts. Her eyes held grateful tears.

"She's wowing them," Mort muttered.

As host of the Report on Reports, Ron introduced each participant by doing somersaults to and from the podium on the stage.

There was a mime who did a Report on Physical Inventory, then a clown who did the Financial Report, a juggler who did The Service Sector, and finally it was Paulina's turn, the Report on Previous Reports.

She wore a long black gown with long black sleeves. She walked silently mid-stage and turned her back to the audience, which caused an uncertain snicker.

The stage had been prepped by the janitorial staff, which had set up pneumatic risers and small beams of light shooting up and out.

Janitors, secretaries, cleaning women, mail clerks and cafeteria workers stepped forward as the rear black curtain rose. They moved in straight lines and broke apart to form a large slow V on stage. Then the risers rose, and they were a chorus.

They sang:

My dreams have changed; why do they haunt me?
Who are these men who never seem to see me?
What happened to the joy I thought was due me?
How did I come here?

The pneumatic risers thrust different questions into the air. Each question or row of singers was answered by another row of singers with another question.

Where is the wonder, the hope?
Why is my heart drawn down at the start of each day?
And my spirit wasted?

They had wonderful voices, both magical and mundane. It was their one chance to ask the questions that bothered them; no one would listen to them again.

They ended:

When I was young, I never thought to come here;
How did I come here?

At the last word the risers in their various positions descended, and the spotlights went off scattershot, like ducks being hit at a midway.

"Lights up! Lights up!" Ron shouted, rushing out with his arms raised. He beamed broadly, as if he knew quite well what everyone was thinking. "Weren't they terrific?" he cried insincerely. "But my, my, my, weren't they a downer?" He winked broadly. "And wouldn't you know it—it couldn't come at a better time—the next one up is Manny Gomerson with his Judgement on the Reports. How we doin', Manny?"

And to Paulina's dismay (she hadn't known their performances would be rated), Manny came out in a full-fledged tuxedo with a bunch of large interoffice envelopes in his hand. "Oh, that one wasn't good for morale," Manny stated, shaking his head and rolling his eyes. "I mean, this is a job, right, not a psychiatrist's couch. But enough philosophizing—let's get down to work. We have seven prizes and eight Reports. How should we do this, Ron? Everyone made a great effort, and they all deserve prizes, but we don't have enough to go around. We have to do some eliminating, okay? Can I have everyone up front?"

Mort patted Paulina on the shoulder—a loser's pat, Paulina thought glumly.

As the last one off the stage she was the first to go back on, and lined up with Mindy, the mime, the juggler, two clowns, a baton twirler and a man who did a swing dance with a manikin. "They're all going to win and I'm going to lose," Paulina thought. She told herself that winning didn't matter, that she had wanted to show off the truth and beauty of the chorus—but the chorus was huddled in the wings with disappointed faces.

"Only the first two rows vote," Manny warned (those rows were reserved for bosses). "You just send in a number on your cell phones (everyone's got a line to the Tally Committee now, right?). One to ten, ten the best. Here we go!"

The audience cheered and booed with absolute abandon. Ron encouraged it, striding across the stage like Groucho Marx and stopping to hold his hand over someone's head for the vote. "Mimes are in a revival," he shouted. "They're kitschy, they're quaint. But we still hate them, don't we?" And the audience roared. They roared for Mindy ("Who knows what she said? Look at that dress!") and the juggler ("Have you ever tried it? Start with eggs.") It was obvious that the crowd was roaring at Ron, not the performers, because he got to Paulina and said, "We all appreciate the effort involved for everyone concerned, let's give them a hand," and the crowd clapped politely but unenthusiastically until Ron added, "For the anti-Hallelujah chorus." Cheers and catcalls rang out.

A phone rang onstage and Ron picked it up. "We have our winners!" he shouted, holding up the envelopes, and he named everyone but Paulina. "Congratulations, all!" he crowed. "Your contract is renewed for another year."

Paulina stood empty-handed. "Contract? I never had a contract."

Ron rushed forward. "Which brings me to our latest announcement. As of today, all Report positions will be contracted out on a competitive basis. Sorry, Paulina, your bid lost."

Paulina's heart was sinking in full view. "Bid? Bid? I don't know what you're talking about."

"You didn't think you had your job forever, did you?" Ron asked with theatrical sympathy, and turned to the crowd. "Who thinks they have their jobs forever?" The crowd booed. "See?" he said, turning back to her. "It's just the times we live in. The times require sacrifice."

The crowd cheered. Ron raised his hands and shook them together. "The party's over!" he said. "Your jobs are all secure." The audience applauded and laughed and began to leave their seats. He turned to Paulina as Mindy came over to join them.

"Well, that was utterly fantastic," Mindy said, linking her arm with Ron's (was Mindy now on Ron's level?).

"We're both very impressed." She raised her eyebrows to show how impressed she was.

There was something familiar about those eyebrows, Paulina thought. "Those are my eyebrows!" she cried. She rubbed her hand above her eyes: nothing!

"Did you hear her?" Mindy asked, laughing. "Did you hear how odd she is? I think she'd make a good comic, much better as a comic than as a whatever she is. What is she? I forget. Oh that's right!" she smacked her head lightly. "You lost."

"She worked in the blah-blah department," Ron said. "Which is due for restructuring."

"Well, she *does* have a creative approach." Mindy said, cocking her head at Ron.

"A good sense of humour, too. Or is it drama?" His face got furrowed. "Was that comedy or tragedy and do we care?"

"No one cared," Mindy said. "Why should they? But no hair, no eyebrows—will it upset the employees?" She took a quick glance over her shoulder to look sympathetically at Paulina.

"Everything upsets the employees," Ron said resignedly.

"So they need cheering up. They need to laugh. I can see her as someone who would give us all a laugh."

"That's true. We could maybe do something with her."

"Wait!" Paulina cried. It was painful, standing there as she was discussed. She had thought her chorus was terrific; she had dreamt of praise about it. How had she been so out of touch? There was a nakedness she felt now, her scalp bald under the wig, her face bald out in the world.

"But she won't need a desk, will she?" Mindy said,

ignoring her. "Comics don't sit at desks, that would be silly."

Ron frowned. "But wouldn't silly actually be the idea?"

"No," Mindy said. She shook her hair, Paulina's hair. She raised her eyebrows, Paulina's eyebrows. "Desks make things look important. That kills the laugh."

"You always get straight to the crux," Ron said.

"So here's the story," Mindy said, turning to Paulina. "You've been fired from your position—or, to avoid lawsuits, actually, your position's been fired in response to the economic slowdown. You're just collateral. But because we care—"

"We always care—"

"We're going to make you a mopper. You mop things up. You keep your salary, you keep your hours, but you have to mop floors."

"In a clown suit?" Ron asked eagerly.

"Just a clown nose, don't you think? We don't want to overdo it."

"In a clown nose, then."

"But wait," Paulina said, clenching her hands. "You can't do this. I don't want to mop floors. I was a supervisor." She heard herself and marvelled at how quickly she had been transformed. "I *am* a supervisor."

"Mopping floors is an important position. Essential, even. Just think of all the used gum there. Someone could get hurt."

"You'll be doing a service to humanity," Ron added. "You'll bring joy and relief to life. That's the company motto, isn't it?" Ron turned to Mindy.

"We have a company motto?"

"This isn't what I want!" Paulina cried. "My message

was to elevate the masses! I never meant to be one!"

"Oh, message," Mindy said dismissively. "Look around you—everyone has left you here alone. They just wanted a little time to vent. That's all they ever do, really: vent and nod and go back to work. You just took yourself a little too seriously. Too personally; you took yourself too personally."

"It's because you stole my hair," Paulina said, pointing her finger at Mindy. "You provoked it."

"Nonsense. People lose their hair all the time. Strand by strand. You really can't claim those hairs as yours once they leave your head, can you? Besides, once you start mopping, you can keep all the hairs you want."

"That's obvious." Ron said agreeably.

"Anyone's hair," Mindy added. "Mine if you want. Just gather it up."

"That, plus you get to keep your paycheque."

"That's what's important in the long term, isn't it? Much more important than hair or where you sit or if you've got great eyebrows? A paycheque."

They began to walk away and Paulina was motionless, considering what had happened. She had gone too far, it was obvious. Asked questions of the wrong people and pushed where a push would be noticed. Such consequences were predictable, to everyone but her. She had expected too much; she thought she could stay hidden in the herd even as she ran along outside it. She was amazed at her own stupidity, grateful that she had been spared the final blow. She would take what they gave her, gratefully.

She did still have a future, after all, she told herself. She was alive. She had bills to pay, many bills to pay, and no savings worth noting. She should accept the position and begin to save money so she could protect herself; why had she cared about protecting others when they could either save themselves or perish? It would be humiliating at first, mopping around her former coworkers, who would, no doubt, shift their eyes away when they saw her. But soon enough it would be normal, even if a new kind of normal.

She had been misled by details, but she could paint on eyebrows, she supposed. She could even paint on hair. Maybe she would get a pair of eyeglasses, just to give her a sense of her new self. She would absolutely refuse the clown nose. She even suspected they were joking about it, proposing it just so they could show how easy it was for them to compromise by removing the request just to please her.

And it would please her!

The mops, she supposed were in the basement.

She turned around and headed there, quickly.

ORDINARY

Guy and Jill were girl-twins, although Guy, of course, was male. Jill was the firstborn, hence the generic "female," despite the genetic "male." Their mom, a sporadic feminist, was in a highly political state following their birth. "Fraternal twins?" she scoffed. "Not these two." Categories are essentially arbitrary, she reasoned. Guy, however, always resented it.

"You ain't gonna girlify me when I grow up," he declared on his sixth birthday. Jill, being bigger, smacked him solid and, although they were close despite their differences, he bit her nose.

"Nice girls!" their mommy yelled. "Nice girls don't do that!" She was a humming kind of woman, tuneless and cheerful; already at six they wanted earphones. "What's that *noise*?" Guy would wail; "What's that *buzzing*?" Jill would cry.

They were signally unrepressed. They acted out all day. They were separated at school—at first by rows and then by floors, but the authorities ("There's something off about those two!") finally discreetly asked if medication might be better.

"God no," their mother said. "Can you imagine them on drugs?"

They were placed in a special school, where they got in trouble by inventing games.

"See, everything we do is made ordinary by one thing," Guy said.

"And if you don't do that one thing, people get creeped out," Jill elaborated. "And it's not normal anymore, when you change one little thing. Like, we come to school, we sit down, we learn. What's the normal thing to do?" she asked Robbie and Cheryl and Gus.

"Coming to school!" Gus crowed.

Guy shook his head. "Sitting down. If we don't do that, it's not normal."

And it was true. The next day word had spread to all the special kids and when the teacher began class, the children stood. They mostly didn't even giggle (Gus did, of course). The teacher, an old hand, played along and started teaching anyway, but lapsed into staring when they began walking around up and down the rows, eerily silent.

Everyone had to stay after school, but they agreed it was worth it. As punishment they had to clap their hands for an hour. It was a progressive special school.

"You children are too damn smart, and it's all my fault," their mother complained after yet another visit to the principal. "Too much protein in your early years, it was all the rage. Now it's all spinach and kale, if only I'd known!" She fell down in an apoplexy of shame, her face on her forearm, her long, long hair in a pigtail to her waist. She would never cut her hair, she said, it was a woman's strength. They'd have to sneak up behind her and tie her down before she'd let her power go like that.

The children cut the leaves off trees, put the wheels sideways on their friends' skates, and insisted on eating alphabetically: apples, artichokes, almonds on Monday, bananas, butterscotch and beans on Tuesday, and, "Cake, cake, cake!" they screamed on Wednesday. Coconut cake, chocolate cake, custard cakes and more. At least it wasn't protein, their mother thought. Wednesday was followed by donuts, dillweed and dipsy-doodles. They liked it, the alphabet, it was working out fine.

"Don't expect much when you get to the *X*s," their mother warned. "And you know, with Z, all we can eat is zoup!" She liked the game, being deeply suspicious by then of any nutritional standards.

They grew up addicted to trouble and attention, though they never went with the trends. No drugs, alcohol or speeding cars: those things were anonymous. And they had a wicked sense of fun. Once, Guy was arrested for running down a Canada goose, a protected species. The police came to his door, citing an eyewitness, and led him back to the scene. There was a chalk outline of a goose in the middle of the road.

"I did not commit goosicide!" Guy yelled, falsely sobbing. "I am not a goosicide!" And then he broke down totally. "It goosed me! I had to do it! I didn't stand a chance. How many times could I let it goose me? My wife is gone, my dog is ashamed, it was an accident."

"Office, officer," the eyewitness said, running out from the sidelines and looking suspiciously like Jill, "it wasn't an accident, he ran it down deliberately. I saw it all, it was a wild-goose *chase*."

Guy's eyes rolled in pseudo agony. "It turned its back

on me and walked all loosey-goosey under my brakes. How much can a man take?"

The police officers had been silent, but now they rallied. One went to answer his squawker and the other one said, "Are you crazy, the two of you, or is this a joke? I'm here to tell you: it'll be better if you're crazy."

"We got our drugs crossed," Jill said brightly. "We're not responsible for any of this, though technically and legally we can still drive."

"That was the morgue," the other officer said on his return. "It's been dead over a day. They think a dog did it, anyway, not a car."

"Ho, ho, ho," his partner said grimly. "False reports. Embarrassing an officer. Let's goose-step these two over to the station."

They were made to do community service, cleaning golf courses of goose crap. "And don't do nothing freaky with it," they were told by an officer who knew them. "That stuff's loaded with carcinogens."

Which was all they needed to dress in latex gloves and fitted plastic bags. Guy especially was critical of carcinogens because he believed they would thin his hair.

For, truth be told, both of them were a little vain and a little flamboyant. They had an idea in their heads of their personal style, which was unique, trend setting even if the trend didn't follow, and of course attractive and complementary. When Jill shaved her head, Guy wore wigs. When Guy penciled his eyebrows, Jill pierced her itty-bitty toe.

"Will you wear a ring on your toe in winter?" Guy asked.

"It's for sandals only. And you know, I can draw a

ribbon or a thong through the hole and wrap it around my ankle or my leg."

Guy got his own itty-bitty toe pierced so they could thread a thong from her toe to his, Siamese twins joined at the corns, but it ripped the hole clear through on Jill's toe and made walking impossible. That was no good. They were not much for just standing around.

They were desperate for sensation, for the new, the first, the only. They clicked their fingernails impatiently on days where nothing clicked in their brains.

And so they reached adulthood, stopping and starting, running hot and cold. They were terribly disappointed that this was all there was.

"I feel so flat today," Jill sighed one evening. "I feel like a cardboard sign, the kind you never notice 'cause you've seen it a thousand times."

"What are we supposed to do with life?" Guy agreed. "Going to school every day never worked, and now we're supposed to work every day. How do people do that?"

"I don't care *how*," Jill said sulkily. "But why, why, why? Don't they feel so carbon working like that?"

"All in a row," Guy snorted. "Machines, pigeons, one mirror after the other." He was silent, his fingers twitching at the air. "I'd collapse like a balloon. I wonder how they get so flat and just keep going. Doesn't it needle them? Don't you think it annoys them to be so organized?"

"I'm not sure they're the same as us," Jill countered sadly. "They're placid, they're like pictures of themselves—an inch deep really; less than an inch. Walking around, getting cracked at the knees." She sat on the sofa next to her brother and put her head on his thigh. "I like looking at you from this angle. I wish I could draw; I'd do a portrait like this."

"Any way you can draw is good enough," he said, brightening. "Do it. Do it now."

She couldn't find a pencil, so she did it in ballpoint pen on the back of an envelope. The thinning dark hair, slightly wavy, cut-glass cheekbones, a somewhat snobby nose. "It's done," she said, frowning.

"Is that how you see me?" He was disappointed.

She held the envelope by its flap and disowned it. Her fingers formed an *O*. "No. I just have no talent at all."

"How *do* you see me?"

"You got coloured outside the lines," she said. "You're bigger than life. And maybe a little bit crazy."

"I don't feel crazy," he said. "Not right now. Do you ever think, maybe you don't exist?"

She sprawled out again on the sofa, resting her head on his thigh. When she had no plans she could get very languid. "Sometimes, but mostly I wonder if other people really exist. You know, am I dreaming or pretending they're there? Then I think, my dreams wouldn't be so dull, and these people are dull. And they annoy me, the way they look at me sometimes, or *don't* look at me, just knock me out of the way with their elbows. People and their damn elbows. They should look up and see me more than they do, I could scream."

He nodded. "They don't have anything in their brains, it's so easy to trick them. Even the tricks are no fun, they've ruined that." He looked at her. "I wonder if I could trick *you*."

Her hands, usually so mobile, froze. "We think too much alike, how could we do it? And why? What would you prove?"

"I'm terribly bored," he said. "And now there's no money. I still think mom should have done the decent thing and died quickly instead of using up all the money."

"It's over and done with. We need a plan."

There was a way he had of delaying when he had something special in mind, of holding it like a candy in his mouth. He was doing that now; she could tell he had a plan.

"Would you like to be a whore?" he said, as if he were asking, "Would you like a cup of tea?"

"Huh," she said, and got a little distracted. The pupils got dark and deep, he saw, as if she were looking at something in a different room. The skin on her neck caught a shadow from her chin; it looked like a line across her throat. "It's a little—oh, sleazy, isn't it?" Her voice was casual. "It's a little down and dirty, isn't it?" When he let her think about it, not answering at once, she added, "And what about you? Will you do it too?"

"Well, of course I could do it too," he said, suddenly energized. She could feel the muscles in his thigh tighten under her cheek. "I could be one too! It will be degrading, won't it? Shameful and defiant!" He rolled the words in his mouth. "There's all that sensation in it—repulsion, anticipation, greed and curiosity. Maybe even a kind of triumph, a nasty triumph."

"So many of them are kinky," she said softly, "so many of them are strange. They have fetishes, they have little kinky dreams they want played out."

He touched her ear with a finger gracefully arched. "Well, we like fantasy well enough, don't we?"

"We'll be in *their* fantasies this time. And it may be even weirder stuff for you, I don't know. Would you do men or women?"

A little smile pulled at his lips. A small indentation like a fingerprint appeared next to his mouth. "Does it matter? No, if I started, it wouldn't matter. We could work together sometimes, the two of us, offer ourselves as a couple."

She flushed; it was odd to see her do it, she was never embarrassed. "Yes, once we start it, I suppose we could."

"I would like to be frightened," he said softly. "Totally frightened. All your senses pick up then, even if you don't notice at the time. And you don't notice, do you? You're so much you, you're a hyper-real you. The way your nerves jump all over the place, and your eyes and head are watching for every clue. Your skin prickles, your palms sweat, even your hair. . . . You don't notice you're living until it seems you won't, and then each breath counts, each shake of the heart." He ended on a whisper.

"I'm not all that crazy about being frightened," Jill murmured. She opened the fingers of her hand and watched them spread and relax. Then her hands curled up. "If you're frightened, then someone controls you. I don't care for that. I don't want to be controlled. But I want to see what happens—I mean, I like it when someone else is frightened, to see how they look, to see what they do. Some get pale, some get flushed, and you can hear it when they speak, they sort of pant. I would hate to hear that in my own voice. I don't mind seeing their fantasies, their screwy little desires, that's okay, they need me for that. I want to see them exposed, it's the only time I can stand them. I like them better when they're raw, stripped down. I could even love them, then, when their voices get so very narrow. They watch me, they have to watch me. I like that focus."

He admired the picture she had of herself. As far as he knew, it was true. "You wouldn't ever feel humiliated, would you?"

"Not if I have the whip hand." She tapped him gently. "You want to be pushed to the edge; I can see that. The edge is very beautiful. But you don't need them for that; they'd be no good, they'd never understand. They don't have the mind for it, for real fear; they're not special enough to give you what you want. They're afraid of small things and that's what they deal in. Most of them, anyway."

"What about you?" he whispered. "If I asked, would you make me afraid?"

"Ah, Guy," she said softly. "I don't know. Would you be the same to me after that? Would I be the same to you?"

He flung himself off the sofa and stretched. "I'm not against change. I can't go on like this much longer." He became suddenly businesslike. "We have to find out where to go. We'll have to get *things*, too, I suppose—condoms and gels; special clothes; shoes; masks; I want masks."

"Masks," she agreed.

"And you—feathers? Lace? Black or red?" He stood by the side of the window, against the frame, so he had a silhouette. His head turned to her from within the shadow.

"Red, I think. Are we really going to do this?"

"Can you think of a reason not to?"

She bent at the waist and grasped her ankles and released them. He suspected she had a scene revolving in her head. "Would you kill someone?" she asked.

He came back to her slowly and very gracefully.

They both felt that the air had thickened around them, around them exclusively. "I don't know; I think about it, of course. Doesn't everyone think about it? Wonder if they could do it, when they would do it, under what circumstances. And if they would do it out of curiosity. You read about joy-killings and you think, those people are off, they don't realize it, they're missing something fundamental the rest of us have. And then I wonder: do I have it? Maybe I don't; would I want it? Wouldn't I prefer to be someone who could kill in cold blood, indifferently? After all, killing out of passion or self-preservation is hardly killing at all. I couldn't kill a stranger, it would have to be someone I loved. That's the real strength, isn't it; that's ultimate power, to be above the things you love or want, to master indifference on that scale. How else can you be truly alive?"

"So you would kill someone," she said meditatively.

"I'm not sure; I like to think I would. What about you?"

"No," she said, and she could tell he was disappointed.

"You can't even imagine doing it, can you?" he asked. He was extremely annoyed; he had thought she would feel exactly as he did.

"Oh I can imagine it; I *have* imagined it. But doing it is another thing. I would stop there."

"And who have you imagined killing?" he asked, surprised.

"You." She watched him carefully. "To think how it would be without you. To be away from you."

He considered this for a long time, letting the idea of it creep around them like an odour. He imagined the look on her face—raising a knife, cocking a pistol, surely it would be sudden?—and he moved the expression around, making it subtler, broader, combining it with satisfaction, lust, regret. These went rapidly through his head, but there were so many variations that the silence lengthened and enriched itself. And how would he feel, seeing her face (now dark with fury, now pale with nerves) and the weapon pointed at him, the moment centrifugal to him; how hard would his heart beat, his palms sweat; would his knees weaken or his hands shake; what would he see, what would he feel? He was aroused.

She laid her hand on his lap, but neither of them moved past that. They sat there, their breaths quickening, the air in the room filled with shadowy expectant figures— writhing, stalking, crying out.

LANDSCAPE, WITH FISH

"You gotta control your fish better," Willis said. "They're scaring my dog."

Tom nodded. "Didn't know they could go so far. It's interesting."

"The first time, yes," Willis agreed. "After that, it's nasty. The dog ain't the same."

"Easy now, it's just a fish."

"I hear they eat things you wouldn't think. I hear they slide right under doors."

"That ain't true, about the doors. You're thinking of mice, not fish. These fish eat mice, so they're more like cats. Only not so fast, I think. At least, I haven't seen 'em move that fast."

"I hear," Willis said slowly, "I hear they can get in the pipes. You know, you're sitting on the john . . ."

"Now that's damn foolish," Tom said. "That's maligning my fish."

"Keep 'em on a leash," Willis said flatly. "And put up some kind of fence."

"It's a good thing we're friendly," Tom said shortly. "Or I'd be annoyed." With that, Tom lowered his head and left. He came across one of those special-order fish of his on the well-worn path back to his own house, and he kicked it a little. It made a kind of hissing sound.

"You watch it," he said to the fish. "You were meant to be eaten, you know." He looked at the fish, its big toothy mouth, its snaky head. "Though I wouldn't want to see you on my plate. Not without gravy, anyway."

He poked the fish back to the pond and set to putting up a fence around it. "Fencing a pond," he grumbled. "Damn foreign fish."

He pounded in the posts and put up the mesh. The fish sort of hopped along the ground so it didn't have to be high. The job went easily.

He thought it was his imagination when he heard the pops against his window in the morning. He sat at the kitchen table and had his coffee first; that was his rule. He saw movements, like big flies, out of the side of his eyes, but he waited to catch them dead-on.

He saw one, finished his coffee, saw another, and got up.

They were leaving oval slimy smears on the windows and falling in the bushes around the house. A little stunned they were, obviously shook up 'til they got their wits about them again. It annoyed Tom when he saw them, because it meant there'd be trouble. He didn't have the kind of neighbours that would let a thing like this go by without comment.

He never actually saw them take off—he always caught them flying, instead—but he had to assume they did a kind of leap first, so he put up a higher fence.

That didn't stop them, and his windows were getting all smeared. Well, then, some kind of tent would do it.

He stared at his little pond, which, when you started thinking about covering it, got a whole lot bigger. He sighed. It might be best if he got Willis to help him. It was hardly a secret he could keep.

Kind of strange he hadn't heard from Willis anyway, he thought, as he walked the old path to his neighbour's house. There were fish in the trees and they sometimes dropped on top of him with a wet thwack and an unpleasant snapping of teeth. They hadn't quite got the hang of it yet; they landed upside down and their teeth went nowhere.

Willis' place was looking a little off. The grass must have gone to seed because there was a whole flock of grackles standing off to the side making grackly cackles.

"Psst," Willis said, tapping on his window from inside. "Get in here."

Tom stepped inside.

"No problems getting through?" Willis whispered. "You didn't hear anything?"

Tom frowned. "Well, there's birds outside. I did hear that."

Willis drew in a long breath. "What were they saying?"

With that, Tom started to actually listen to the murmur outside, which wasn't exactly the regular kind of bird talk. He stepped to the window. The birds were walking around, meeting in groups. He listened hard.

The birds were saying, "WILLIS Willis Willis. WILLIS Willis Willis."

He stepped away from the window. "Now, that's creepy," he said.

Willis nodded. "Did they say anything about you?"

Tom listened again, but there was nothing but Willis

in the air. "No," he said. "It's just you."

"What if they start lying?" Willis asked. "Won't nobody believe me over birds." His eyes got filmy. "How much do you think they know?"

Tom went out down the path and picked up a few of his fish. It seemed like they'd followed him part way. Some fish hopped along behind him back to Willis' place, and when he got to the grackles one fish reared up and grabbed a bird by the wing. Tom kicked it free, watching that bird rise up and join the others scattering overhead. As long as they were talking, they could talk about that.

Willis peeked from his window until the yard was clear and then he came out. "Those fish of yours," he said. "Mighty evil looking. They got a temper?"

"Sweet as can be," Tom said. "They get attached, too, just like a dog."

"I think my dog ran out on me. Kind of miss him."

They stood for a while in silence, watching the fish. They were flapping on the ground, wiggling their tails back and forth till they started making a bunch of holes around the yard. Then they each settled into a hole and turned their heads towards the two men by the house.

"Well," Tom said. "Looks like they're planning on staying. You want 'em?"

Willis nodded. "I can see their attraction now. They'll keep the yard free anyway. And they're quiet—I like that."

Tom nodded. "Real quiet," he said. "You never hear them coming. You never know they're there."

Satisfied, the two men looked at the fish, and the fish in their trenches looked back at them.

PUBLICATION HISTORY

"FishWish," originally published in *Weird Tales*, Winter 2011.

"The Inner City" originally published in *Cemetery Dance*, February 2008.

"Down on the Farm" originally published in *Bandersnatch*, PrimeBooks, 2007.

"The Great Spin" originally published in *Confrontation Magazine*, Winter 2010; and *Wet Ink magazine*, September 2009.

"The Escape Artist" originally published in *International Quarterly*, 1997.

"The Large People" originally published in *Daily Science Fiction*, July 2011.

"After Images" originally published in *Phantom*, Prime Books, 2009.

"Creating Cow" is original to this collection.

"Beds" originally published in *Moon Milk Review*, February 2010.

"How Lightly He Stepped in the Air" originally published in *Short Fiction by Women*, Issue 4.

"The Difficulties of Evolution" originally published in *Weird Tales*, June/July 2008.

"Thick Water" originally published in *Albedo One Magazine*, Spring 2011.

"The Hair" originally published in *Michigan Quarterly Review*, Spring 2011.

"Ordinary" originally published in *Confrontation Magazine*, Spring/Summer 2002.

"Landscape, with Fish" originally published in *Weird Tales*, February 2008.

ABOUT THE AUTHOR

Karen Heuler's stories have appeared in over sixty literary and speculative journals and anthologies, including several "Best of" collections. She's published a short story collection and three novels, and won an O. Henry award in 1998. She lives in New York with her dog, Philip K. Dick, and her cats, Jane Austen and Charlotte Bronte. Website: www.karenheuler.com

EMB
RACE
THE
ODD

GOLDENLAND PAST DARK

CHANDLER KLANG-SMITH

A hostile stranger is hunting Dr. Show's ramshackle travelling circus across 1960s America. His target: the ringmaster himself. The troupe's unravelling hopes fall on their latest and most promising recruit, Webern Bell, a sixteen-year-old hunchbacked midget devoted obsessively to perfecting the surreal clown performances that come to him in his dreams. But as they travel through a landscape of abandoned amusement parks and rural ghost towns, Webern's bizarre past starts to pursue him, as well.

AVAILABLE MARCH 2013

978-1-927469-35-4

ZOMBIE VERSUS FAIRY FEATURING ALBINOS

JAMES MARSHALL

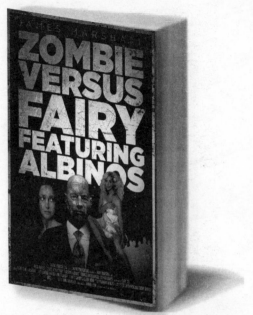

In a PERFECT world where everyone DESTROYS everything and eats HUMAN FLESH, one ZOMBIE has had enough: BUCK BURGER. When he rebels at the natural DISORDER, his marriage starts DETERIORATING and a doctor prescribes him an ANTI-DEPRESSANT. Buck meets a beautiful GREEN-HAIRED pharmacist fairy named FAIRY_26 and quickly becomes a pawn in a COLD WAR between zombies and SUPERNATURAL CREATURES. Does sixteen-year-old SPIRITUAL LEADER and pirate GUY BOY MAN make an appearance? Of course! Are there MIND-CONTROLLING ALBINOS? Obviously! Is there hot ZOMBIE-ON-FAIRY action? Maybe! WHY AREN'T YOU READING THIS YET?

AVAILABLE MAY 2013

978-1-77148-141-0

THE 'GEISTERS
DAVID NICKLE

When Ann LeSage was a little girl, she had an invisible friend—a poltergeist, that spoke to her with flying knives and howling winds. She called it the Insect. And with a little professional help, she contained it. But the nightmare never truly ended. As Ann grew from girl into young woman, the Insect grew with her, becoming a thing of murder.Now, as she embarks on a new life married to successful young lawyer Michael Voors, Ann believes that she finally has the Insect under control. But there are others vying to take that control away from her. They may not know exactly what they're dealing with, but they know they want it. They are the 'Geisters. And in pursuing their own perverse dream, they risk spawning the most terrible nightmare of all.

AVAILABLE JUNE 2013

978-1-77148-143-4

978-1-926851-67-9
SANDRA KASTURI &
HALLI VILLEGAS (EDS)

IMAGINARIUM 2012

978-1-926851-
NICK MAMATAS

BULLETTIME

978-1-926851-69-3
PAUL TREMBLAY

**SWALLOWING A
DONKEY'S EYE**

978-1-97469-10-1
JOHN PARK

JANUS

978-1-927469-09-5
DANIEL A. RABUZZI

**THE INDIGO
PHEASANT**

978-1-927469-16-3
IAN ROGERS

**EVERY HOUSE IS
HAUNTED**

978-1-927469-21-7
ROBERT SHEARMAN

**REMEMBER WHY
YOU FEAR ME**

978-1-927469-
HELEN MARSHALL

HAIR SIDE, FLESH SIDE

978-1-927469
ROBERT BOYCZUK

**THE BOOK OF
THOMAS: HEAVEN**

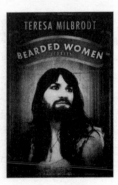

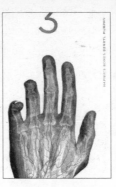

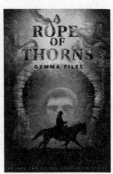